Debris: Stories

Daniel
S.C.
Sutter

Debris

winner of the Press 53 Award for Short Fiction

Press 53
Winston-Salem

Press 53, LLC
PO Box 30314
Winston-Salem, NC 27130

First Edition

Cover design by Claire V. Foxx

Library of Congress Control Number
2026936301

ISBN 978-1-968783-04-4

For my mother

Contents

Like Always Blooming

In '93, a month after Yankee Jim Abbott, born without a right hand, threw a no-hitter and fooled me into believing baseball could bring us back together, I signed divorce papers. My wife left for Florida with a man who took fire back in Desert Storm. He'd been teaching aerobics at the Y.

My wife got the dog, Polaris. As in the brightest of stars. I got our thirteen-year-old daughter, Blossom. As in what clementine flowers do. Sure, I'd been unfaithful first, a few times. I'd given my sorries as best I could.

Now she and her guy were off for the beaches and tides and coolers of icy longnecks. My little girl and I stayed put in New Orleans. There was no ocean sand, but our air carried better colors from the oil and grease of perseverance. I held a mortgage on a house against the Mississippi. One day it'd be worth something, I told everyone—though nature would claim it soon enough. Still, Blossom chose me and the city. Fall loomed, and the girl had two more games to pitch.

I stirred a pot of mac and watched Blossom, lanky like me, through the window. She allowed a hug from her mother, then swatted away a blown kiss as my wife rode away. At the table, I waited for Blossom to speak on it, but she didn't say a word about sadness. She ate with her hands. "Who do you think wins the Series this year, Hoss?" she said.

"Cardinals," I said. "Could be the Cardinals."

Blossom applied a smear of cheese under each eye and stared me down as if calling for the put-away pitch. "I like the Braves."

"Yeah, you and all the rest."

"In five," she said and gave me that smile you'd be lucky to have even one person grant you in this life.

I let her stay up past Letterman, and when she fell asleep, I stretched Blossom's legs across the sofa to cover her with a blanket and cleaned her face with a dishcloth.

She kept her room as tidy as her mother kept the house, so her prayer journal was easy to find. Not under the pillow, not even in the drawer of her desk, but instead right on the bedside table beneath a lamp left on. A pinky promise had restricted me from the words inside for years, but there are times a father is allowed his child's secrets. No entries of substance, though, nothing of the divorce or her mother or me or the sight of a dog scared from so much shouting—only wishes for a couple more friends, fewer red marks on her exams, and a lower earned run average. But from under the binding pocket poked an envelope marked a few months before and signed with love from the man who took fire in Desert Storm. Inside, a picture card. Images of batting cages, pitching nets, candids of cleats rounding third and churning up dust.

Fall training in Tampa, read the scrawl from a pencil. *Starts in August and lasts till January. All girls and only girls. You'll love it.*

Blossom leaving. The possibility. The immense pain in that likelihood.

With despair I tried to rip the paper to bits, but my strength couldn't match my heart. I placed it on the ledge of her window where she wouldn't miss that I now owned more information than she'd been willing to share. I left the door open on the way out to dare her to give me the skinny with her own volition. Face-to-face.

I sat on the carpet and against the sofa in case Blossom woke to cry or to finally ask about all of those little, accumulated things I'd gathered. The penances I deserved—like when her mother let loose a snake in my shower, like when her mother took a cheese grater to my backside. Like that time, years ago, I yelled at Blossom too loudly for scraping crayons across the wall only to realize she'd drawn an image of me smiling. "It's you saying everything will be not so sad soon," she'd said, and my heart was dented. But now, around the time the morning birds seized the powerlines, Blossom shook me awake and pointed to a fried egg on the counter.

"We got work," she said. The tightest braid I'd ever seen. The dirtiest, clay-stained socks. "You a skipper, or no?"

"I'm a skipper," I told her.

Blossom said, arm over head for a stretch, "Or maybe you're a skip who sneaks through my things."

Scolded, I guess I found some tears on *my* face, whatever. I wiped my cheeks and followed her out. "I am still a father, also."

I knocked her some come-backer balls down the levee. A spilling cloud grazed the east, but otherwise skies like airport postcards. A bouncer ricocheted off an ant pile, and somehow Blossom scooped it in stride. Fresh glove. True leather. Boar-black and purchased right before she picked me over her mother.

Two more slow rollers and Blossom finally stopped for a breath.

"Boys on the teams are starting to look me over, Big Dog," she yelled and spit a big sticky a few yards uphill.

I said back, "Hey, maybe don't get into all that yet."

"Why?"

I jogged toward her so no one alive could hear the conversation.

"Because," I said, "it's a dirty business, that."

"You're a silly one." She reached to pat my shoulder and left a handprint on my sleeve. "Long as they're watching my ass and not my windup, I come out the benefactor."

"You hear that from your mother?" I said.

"Benefactor?" she said.

"No, not benefactor." A stray dog chased the sound of a practicing trumpet coming from over the railroad tracks. "Watching *ass*," I said.

"You'd be surprised, Honcho." She winked and motioned me backward. "I hear a lot from you, too."

I sliced the next three balls into the river, and out of frustration, I smashed the fourth in the direction of the faraway trumpet. Pop. High and hard. And there goes the girl.

A confession.

At sixteen I stole the service dog of a blind man and drove it to the swamps and tall grass of the Gulf, fifty miles south of New Orleans. I'd never met either, the blind man or the Doberman. But they lived three trailers down and would cry and bark until sunrise. Their wails grew too loud. Then their wails grew louder. Explosions. Maybe lonely, is all, maybe a wife in the ground, distant children, but I was a pitcher then myself—like Blossom, like Jim Abbott—recruited by three schools and making a name. And my arm, the muscles and strings, tendons, the sinews, needed rest. So when I caught them napping on their porch swing, I lured the pet away with a stick of jerky. Left near a bent street pole at river mile marker 2 East, who knows how long it waited for anyone who'd drive that deep before choosing which direction to run.

I blew my next three starts, and the man spent months calling for his companion, tripping on cracked sidewalks and his own metal stick. I felt bad. Remorse. I said my Hail Marys, but the man died by Christmas, and a ligament ripped itself from my shoulder joint in a way that never healed enough to throw faster than sixty, and I would never pitch another game.

Blossom had practice, so I headed to church to light some candles for more forgiveness, to send up some heat for a little understanding. I left the truck on the curb and figured I'd hop the streetcar like the outsiders do. Rolling uptown and toward the chapel it was jammed, the seats sticky and grimed. I blew away the breaths of passengers, and two old men murmured about the better days of Nixon. A kid with a skateboard across his lap lit a cigarette, and a cluster of nuns in the front rows said *God no* and *to hell with that*, so he flicked it out the window and spat on the floor.

A man next to me tugged at his bowtie, then eyed me over and placed a finger on his lips. He slid his hand down the ass pocket of a standing woman who gripped the overhead rail, unaware. He removed a greenback, and she sneezed into her arm. "A whole twenty," he mouthed and folded the bill into an airplane. He poked it lightly onto his cheek and whistled Dixie. I didn't judge. I adjusted my watch until the streetcar squealed, stopped.

Outside, a banner day. Spanish moss and old Carnival beads hung from power lines and oak limbs. The smell of sunburnt flowers. Joggers huffing air and a line of strollers gliding, a line of moms pushing.

I followed the nuns, and after two blocks I was stung by the sound of horns and trumpets, brass. A rope blocked the pathway to the cathedral grounds, and the nuns were allowed entry. Food carts sat in rows. Rings were tossed. I shielded the sun with my hand and watched a kid stumble across the grass with a bagged goldfish.

"What's this?" I said.

A bald man extended a hand. "Fundraiser event."

Entry to the fair cost three dollars, and when I made my way past all the parents—men throwing darts for teddys, kids pointing to which one, all licking on creamsicles and shortcake—I found the church doors locked. Greasy from humidity, my nostrils dripped. A clown in a dunk tank shouted me over, and I clenched the air in the instinctive motion of tugging at my mother's skirt in fear, as I did when a child.

"Can't hit the bull's-eye, peckerhead," the clown said and raised his fists.

I kicked at a cricket hiding in the grass blades, and after I paid the fee, I missed the target three times.

"Peckerhead." He pouted through his face paint, and I tried, failed again.

I told him it was only because the nuns were over my shoulder. And they were, bobbing and giggling. I flashed them the rosary from my pocket, and finally they led me around the building, past Saint Thomas Aquinas and through the hedged garden. Here, where Blossom's mother and I stood for wedding poses, snaps, flashes: *Perfect. That's it. Now a little more arm around the waist like the lovebirds you are.*

The sisters pulled me in the back way and stood watching while I knelt in front of the candles. I echoed a cough and lit three. One for my late mother's soul, one for my own mercy, and the one most beautiful, from melting, for Blossom's affection. I bit at my fingernails, crossed myself, and asked the nuns what one should do if one knows himself to be a peckerhead—for instance, if one can intellectualize being such a peckerhead but can't find within himself the necessary implements to achieve emotional growth—asked what a peckerhead does to gain the love of a daughter, not just to gain but to also fortify that love, in a way similar to tying one knot over another knot so as to ensure it does not drift away. What does a peckerhead do, then, to grant however much of that love is left over, yes, to *himself*?

They answered with something, but their syllables blended to a rattle, and overwhelmed, I excused myself too quickly.

With no cash or change left, I hiked it back past the cracked cemeteries and houses with mucked windows.

The sweat felt maybe cleansing. I said to God, *Please and thank You and may I have some more, Sir.*

That afternoon, grayer weather, and with the last out to get, Blossom had Max the suburbanite on a full count. The asshole was plump, and at that age, this meant strong. He kept fouling and skying them to the bleachers. I swallowed whole seeds and shells, right leg shaking. Two rows up from me, a young and tipsy couple wrangled a ball, kissed like they'd found each other's souls. Well congratulations and something blue.

Blossom stepped off the bump, and the opposing dugout chirped about training bras and lesbos, but they were scared. She threw flames and they knew it. Her blood calm, polar. She spoke to the inside of her glove, tugged her earlobe, and resumed position. In Blossom's form, her bending and heel-pivots and that extra length, I saw her mother's refinement and poise.

The pitch was high and tight, calculated risk, and the fat boy swung and whiffed like he was aiming for a wasp nest. Done deal, and Blossom made small show of it. Just a snarl to her antagonists and a finger gun to me. I fired back.

In under ten minutes we met at the truck because she wasn't about to shower with any boys. We bumped elbows.

"Electrolytes, Big Dog," she said. "I need 'em."

She was down two Gatorades by the time we hit traffic on the canal bridge.

"Max says a few league fams are meeting for pizza tonight," Blossom said. "You game or are you game?"

I messed with the rearview mirror. "Didn't you just send him packing?"

"Business is just for the field."

The radio was all-day bluegrass, and I turned it down. "Well," I said, "I guess all right then."

Rain. Wipers.

At home I dressed for the event. I wondered what color shirt looked best on a man who'd lost his wife and, in not many tomorrows, would lose his daughter to another state. How do you speak completely, coherently without stammer, when most of your learned language has closed the door behind it?

"We tried scream therapy in the woods," I told the other parents at the table. I'd thrown back a few beers, and the kids were off smacking pinballs and jamming fingers at air hockey. "That's when you really know you're done. Everything's kaput. When you're up at midnight screaming at air and anthills with your wife, and even the possums take her side."

Some tried to laugh. Some sipped slowly at their sodas and waved for the checks. Most stood to find their children and said it was due time to tuck in. Soon I was down to one other parent. Plump Max's plumper father.

"That Jim Abbott," he said. "God Almighty, bless him."

I fished the lemon wedge from under the ice of my drink and bit for a sting on the tongue.

"Imagine," he continued, "being given that gift. Will and grit. Sonofabitch sure gave the finger to his demons. Overcame them. Overcame the whole damn world." He belched from grease and pepperoni. I needed the toilet.

Blossom stood by the pay phone in the bathroom hallway. Clearly she'd just exchanged words.

"Hoss," she said. "That was Moms on the line. She and her guy, they're proud."

"Why does Max look like he drank Tabasco?" I said. The kid stood down the far end rubbing a red, swollen face. Purple and welted in the morning, for sure.

"Tried to pinch me down the back and below," Blossom said. "Got 'im before the act."

If I'd have been a better parent, maybe I'd have gone for a word with the father.

She said, "It's been a good one, really. But one more game from the mound in this city, and then I got bigger fish."

"To fry?" I said.

"No," she said. "To smack the shit out of."

Max's dad hit the mark on some jackpot game. Here came all the bells and whistles and lights, hoorah.

"Look, I'm going to live with Moms," Blossom said. "League is all girls and only girls for once," she said, using those words of the man who took fire in Desert Storm. "Meant to tell ya. But scared to tell ya."

"I'm aware of this," I said. "I figured this." My left eye twitched, and I held my breath to search for the pulse of her love.

And, sure, it was still present then, that night: Blossom colored for me a picture of Micky Mantle like a child half her age would do. She stuck it, signed and dated, to the fridge. After her bedroom door shut for sleep, I pressed my forehead against the frame and held it there for minutes.

I took a bucket of balls to the levee's top and threw each into the river, trying to match Blossom's form and posture. The aim was off. Everything hooked. So with the last remaining baseball, I reset my feet, in my own way, as they were two decades before when I, too, played her position. Arched spine, head centered, eyes on a curl in the current. Then straighten, left leg lifting. Plant. Release.

While in the throwing, I remembered the moment of conception, the sperm-meets-egg, of what would become my daughter. Someone educated would tell you it's impossible to feel that, but I swear to Jim Abbott I did. Yet another one educated would say it's against the absolutes of science—my wife's left ovary having been removed from a malignant grapefruit and the other withered from chemotherapy. Still, there was an unexpected glowing that night and a beautiful ringing in the ears. The girl, she sang from the onset.

This was the beginning of my faith, for better or worse, godly or not, that I could take what I have done and shatter it for mercy against the wall of improbability.

The momentum took me forward and I tripped. I fell into the muck. The ball didn't even make it to the water. From my belly I watched it roll and pause on the bank's edge, and I pleaded that the anchors of prospect wouldn't moor us all, forever, to where we stand now.

Four afternoons later, Blossom had the bases loaded with one more out to get, only up two runs. She'd walked all three and couldn't find her zone, her lower lip red from biting. She removed her glove and cracked her fingers.

We stood, a big crowd, almost everyone. Max, to my left, his own team eliminated from contention, held his hands clasped over his head, and the nuns whistled and waved their flags from up the bleachers.

"She's got it," Max said. "Like always and forever, she's got it."

I said to shut up and scanned the opposing dugout. Stronger boys from the corn-fed top of the state. Taller and with bigger arms, they all had dyed their hair platinum. Togetherness and that.

Blossom positioned her cleat, dug into the clay. She licked the palm of her right hand and turned her head to the blonds. One yanked at his member and thrusted toward my daughter. Another yelled to ask if she was all sealed down there, if that's why she wouldn't fuck the boys, and no one would want to bang a dyke anyway.

Blossom called for time, turned toward the outfield, and let fall a few tears to the rubber as if to say, too much is too much.

"They've shook her," Max said, and we motioned for the ump, jumped and flailed. I wanted a yards-long arm. I wanted a giant hand. I wanted to reach out and cover her entirely.

She stood to resume and initiated her usual motion. My distraction caught Blossom's eye, and as she let her arm loose, she moved her focus just enough toward me for the ball to curve and ride a flat plane straight into the hitter's swing. Two runs scored, then three.

From the passenger seat, Blossom stared at the crushed cars collected on the back of a big rig. Her sweat wouldn't shut off even with the AC going full. She curled her fingers until each cracked.

"I apologize, I suppose," I said when we pulled off cement and onto gravel. "I promise, yeah, I didn't mean to cause a scene."

"You can stop talking now," she said.

Maybe, days before, I could have let her play some hooky, wooed her, taken her to the batting cages after lunch, and while rehydrating, let in that big elephant—said she was not allowed to go to Florida. It simply wouldn't happen. Demanded. Then perhaps pleaded, possibly. Could've grabbed and shaken her until she knew what I wanted and then wanted the same. Her shoulders would rise, aw shucks, and she'd chuckle like a true child, her true self and true age. Or probably it would hurt her, and in that hurt, she would feel how I felt for once. She would say, *Yes, okay, Daddy, I love you and I'll stay here with you and I'll click through the channels with you and I'll help you stir the chocolate syrup and I'll hold your hand when you well up in the grocery store, Daddy.* She would say that word: *Daddy.*

Or she might come at me big time with the wooden slugger, swinging and telling me to buzz off or she'd bust my nose in, and boy would that leave it crooked. I'd go in for a hug and get a wallop to the stomach. She would vow to never write or call. She'd steal the polaroids. She'd ask what right I have to sympathy, what I deserve. Not love. Not respect. Not even the shiny memories. And certainly not, for a blinking second, her.

But I did not do that. I would not do that. I did not inch close to nudging that fate.

This moment lasted past its time, us together in the cab of my truck, so Blossom put one hand on my shoulder. I whispered that I wouldn't say anything. With her other hand, she shot me the bird.

"You're fine," she told me. "It's just I want to keep slinging the rock." A clamped grip, an old soul shining through. "You're not the best, but you're decent, Hoss," she said. "Tryin' to do all those good dad things and all that good dad shit."

A confession.

Five years out of college and shortly before my wife carried Blossom, I unfaithfully impregnated a sophomore who studied marine biology. Corals, fishes, you name it. We drove to Houston, and I paid 500 for the deed. The girl wore large-framed sunglasses even in the clinic lobby, and on the way back, she undid her seatbelt and told me the brightest thing she'd ever seen was a scale shed off the fin of an angelfish.

From that moment, up through the year of Jim Abbott's no-hitter and the leaving of my daughter, I never visited the ocean, the beach, or any sort of shore. But I think of Blossom now, and I wish I had taken her in search of all the brightest things in all the brightest waters, wish I'd shown her more than baseball—past just sticks and mitts. How to give more than you take, how to take only what you're willing to give. I made a wish I'd still get these chances as Blossom blew at a candle on a grocery store cake, bought the night before her departure to Florida. And the same wish while she dismissed my help and rolled her bags past the attendant, down the terminal. Our finger guns, we shot them.

I stood long at an airport urinal, palm against the wall, so to make my thoughts motionless. On the drive home, while a voice on the radio warned my city of yet another developing weather system, warm and swirling waters, Blossom's plane hovered safely and confidently over the Gulf of Mexico, toward a place of sun-glare and waves and her own ever-infinite potential.

Mantis

Shaken as an infant, abandoned by my father, and squeezed through time and circumstance, I find myself some thirty-odd years later, here, retching onto a frosty hedgerow outside the town house I rent with my mother. I pull myself into focus, and my stomach feels stretched and snapped like a surgeon's glove. This is coastal Florida. Our row of homes sits along the Gulf shore, but it's freezing, so I pretend there's snow and tilt my head to catch an imaginary flake on the tongue, a miracle. An egret on the sidewalk pecks at a worm and fails to kill it. I stamp it out of its misery and grind with the heel. Then, finally, after I stare down the sun, it begins to set for the last time before The Great New Millennium, century twenty-one.

Inside, my mother's on the couch with her boyfriend. The King of Sanitation, they call him. ("You're not customers. You're family.") The two link hands and watch *Jeopardy!*, both wearing their New Year's hats. There's glitter on their brows and on the carpet also.

"You out there for some air, bud?" says The King. "Cold weather to end the year on, but that can be good for you." I don't bother telling him that, no, dumbass, my pharynx is contracting from the fluid produced by an acute anxiety spell. The television goes to static, and he gets up to fidget with the antenna, as he is wont to do these nights he visits.

Mom looks good, rosy and done up for the first time in a while, and that admittedly makes me happy. Her hair bobs above her shoulders. Her lashes are curled long, and she wears a slender-fitting dress that covers one shoulder and exposes the other. For all of last week Mom had worn the same sweatpants, and when she burned her wrist on the oven rack, she spent the rest of the night crying about death and the pearly gates, the inevitability of her struggling ventricles, her failing heart. To help I recited that joke about the Chihuahua and the top hat because she likes that one, but it only worked insofar as she could take a few breaths of calmness.

"We've got those dinner reservations later," she says with tenderness. "We'd both like you to come, get out into the world. Could be back to watch the fireworks over the water after."

I swallow the acid in my throat. "Told you no, but thanks. I have to grade papers."

"School's out for break, my man," The King says. Just like that, he catches the fib and has to remind me of my embarrassing things, throw them in my face: That this PhD is worth a square of toilet paper. That I'm only a history adjunct at the state college, and I am stuck in progress on my book of the Roman emperors. That I don't get offered many classes, and when I do, a lot of them don't even make enough enrollment, so I can't afford a place all my own.

I say I'm headed to my room and touch my mom on the shoulder to signal I love her but I just can't leave the house with this disposition and certainly not with him, The King. She nods because she always tries to understand. We ride the same wavelength. Her style is compassion.

I boot up the computer, and the internet begins to gargle, to dial up. I wait. There's the pornography folder, but my heart's not into it. I'm still thinking of this guy, earlier, who came by in a backpack selling doomsday gear, like radiation goggles and nonperishables. I asked him his deal, and he said that come the year 2000, all the aircraft fall from the sky, the grid fails, the microwaves explode, the chips burn out. He scratched his shin. "Okay," I said. "But what then does this mean for my mother's pacemaker?" He said, "Don't know, broseph. Sorry to say, but she might be a goner," and turned to haul away his batteries and peanuts.

I'm aware of all the apocalyptic speculations—who isn't by now?— and I think of them as absurd and pathetic, but my worry does stay with my mother and that precautionary yet essential electronic machine designed to zap her heart, her fundamental organ.

This sort of panic I now type to Mantis in our private chat so I can get these worries out into the open. I don't have to wait long; she's always online when I need her. I've never seen Mantis in person, but I choose to imagine her as such: a tidy woman my age, her plush visage illuminated by a computer screen in the wet, stone basement of a convent in Rome, perhaps, or at least in some adjacent township. Because of this glowing, one must be able to see the moisture on her upper lip and the tiniest amount of peach fuzz, almost translucent. She will occasionally press her palm down the front of her habit to smooth any wrinkled fabric. Undoubtedly, it's past sleeping hours, and if caught, the reprimand she would receive from the superior would be severe. But I am worth that risk to her.

And for that I am in love, whoever she might actually be.

If all collapses, Mantis says, her text appearing in our chat thread. *You know. How will we communicate without the web? Give me your address now, sweetheart???*

I'm not ready for that, not quite, not yet at the phase of my life for a romance to become tangible. I steer the conversation back to my mother.

But the end of the world, it's not factual or actual, right? I type. *And my mother's pacemaker isn't necessarily needed anyway, right? It's like break-in-case-of-emergency, right?*

I pick at my thumbnail and examine my space, the dinginess in here, the dusty AC vent, the one bulb. And then there's what's taped to the modem: a scrawl written by Mom's fingers on the back of a heart-healthy pamphlet, a poem from her most recent hospital stay. I don't like crying, so I never read any lines except the last one. In heaven or blazing hell, we'll love each other just as well. That's true.

If real, Mantis says, *one startle, and if that heart stops without the machine? She dies??*

Possibly. Yes.

My poor baby, Mantis says because kindness is among her highest virtues. Then a couple beats. *So address yet???* she asks.

The King knocks, opens the door like he's a chum or some kind of dad. "Bud, I want to beg you," he says. "I'll even bribe you if I have to." He tosses his gaudy silver watch onto my bed as an olive branch. "It'll mean the world to your mother if you tag along." I close my eyes but glare at him through my lids, which can be a more potent strategy. "I know it's because of me," The King says. "But it's not like I can back out, can I? Me, you, we're both trying to help her enjoy the simple things while we still have time to." He extends his hairy hand for a shake.

I summon courage. People know of my width but forget my length, so I stand to exist above him. I'm quiet. I spin the ceiling fan blade.

"Okay, I get it," The King says and turns to leave because I have used intimidation. "Keep the watch." I secure The King's timepiece around my wrist, and it suits me well—me in my finery.

I lock the door and feel almost brave enough to give Mantis my address. I type in the coordinates and hover my index above the ENTER key, only to delete without sending. Again, there's the porn folder, and this time I'm feeling it.

Just moments after my culmination there are gunshots—no, firecrackers—outside my window. A group of starlit teens launches the explosives overhead, and I twitch when they ignite above the ocean tide. A wiry kid in a jacket and shorts tosses one of the bombs to his friend, who runs before the bang, before there is damage to any extremities. Their bare feet leave spastic imprints in the sand. The impact zone of their debris inches closer to the marsh end of the beach and toward what they probably can't see in the darkness: my pal Rex's RV, stationed among the sea brush.

I open the window. "Stop it," I whisper, even though I, too, would like such fun. I've never been a good disciplinarian. Cases in point? My students. Occasionally they break my chalk before I arrive to the classroom, as if I were a dunce. They sometimes snicker, heckle my belly. There has been snorting, frightening faces during lectures. I speak toward the floor to prevent any conflict because they are unkind company.

My wall rumbles with the sounds of pipes and faucets, which means Mom or The King or both are showering for dinner. Out of fear of being within earshot of possible intercourse, I slide myself out the window and onto the sand. It triggers the floodlight. I tremble even though I've secured my peacoat, and when I raise my arm to wave at the children, they scatter as if I'm the village ogre.

Rex must've noticed me from his RV. He hobbles out the door and flashes a peace sign to beckon. My left ear rings vaguely, and this is both my anticipation flaring up as well as my tinnitus. My boots conceal my feet and ankles, so as I walk toward Rex's place and look back, my prints appear blocked and mechanical in contrast to the feral steps of the teens.

He pours me something warm and gritty from a blender, and I drink before saying hello because this is our ritual. Rex handles the maintenance in our complex and is the only man I appreciate who's slept with my mother. I just about love him, my only true offline friend. He is nearing seventy. So perhaps due to his tenure, he's accumulated his fair amount of the world's paraphernalia. He's got it all: beanbags, katanas, ashtrays from every state. Books climb from floor to ceiling, wall to wall. He says he's written more than twenty. I can't even complete one.

I give him the brass tacks regarding my mother's artery channels, her shock rhythms, her emergency defibrillator.

"Can't help with your mom, dude," Rex says and pulls me to the space next to him on the sofa. "Been there. Tried that." A calico claws itself onto Rex's lap, then paws at the hair hanging from his chin. "I might be good with appliances but nothing like that, nothing on the inside, all that squishy stuff. Gal's been on her way out for a while, besides."

He pushes away the cat, crosses his legs, and fills a balloon with nitrous. Inhales. I do the same—my self-granted indulgence and as far into the underworld as I'm willing to venture. The gas unscrambles my innards, and for those thirty seconds, all thoughts are fireflies, all worries miasma, far above the ozone.

Rex asks if he can snap a couple photos of me with my arms behind my head, says I'm cute that way. And even though it's odd, I can't help but turn flush and flattered. He takes a few, and I sit again while he winds the camera film.

"I'm no mystic," Rex says. "But this end-of-the-world bullshit might actually hold some merit. Just think of the rhymes: *JFK. Y2K.* And what's the common denominator?" He uses the inside of his shirt collar to blow his nose. "That's right, my dude: the fucking *CIA.*"

"Hmm." I can't blame Rex. Like with the constellations, when there are so many billions of burning suns, how can you not be tempted to connect them all, to sketch the handsomest images to mend the loneliness? "And then there's MLK," I gift him. "But why would the CIA want to kill my mom?"

He palms my knee, massages the top, and then tries to pry at the cap with his index finger. "Why wouldn't they?" he says.

Rex has the shakes of a motor, so he asks if there's any booze at my place and if anyone's home. And, yes, I do have a few bottles in the high drawers, even though The King has recently convinced my mother to stay on the wagon. Rex takes the lead and we exit toward the sand, but out of impulse or kleptomania, I snag the disposable camera he's left on a stack of old newspapers and put it in my coat pocket.

I show Rex in through the front since The King's car is gone for dinner. The heater is buzzing, so I toss my coat on the kitchen counter. I pour him two fingers of some kind of Scotch, and he drinks it like he's sucking on honey. He insists I match him, but it's difficult, I say. It tastes like towering Vesuvius, the metro killer. Rex has no idea what I'm saying—which is nothing, really—but he laughs and lifts himself to kiss my earlobe nonetheless. This is nothing to make a fuss about and far from the first time. He nods toward my room, and as we pass the television, Dick Clark winks at the camera, snow on his shoulders.

My bed is dusty, but we are warm under the quilt. Rex holds my fetal body from behind and reaches for my member. This is as far as it ever goes, and he understands. I am not of that persuasion, I don't think, so I lie un-erected.

After a bit, before I'm asleep, Rex releases his grip and glides his hand over my chest. I am glad for this, Rex's presence, his encompassing, sweaty comfort. I wonder if The King provides this security for my mother. I'm tempted to hope so. Eventually Rex grabs and yanks the hair on the top of my scalp, the wiry bunch barely clinging to the follicles, then exits out the open window, leaving nothing but drool on the pillow.

I load up the instant messenger to check on Mantis's New Year's situation, to see if there's devastation to her time zone, but no response even after seven-plus minutes.

Systems down? I ask. *Send SOS? To what latitude/ longitude???*

I shut my eyes and visualize: Much ruin. Her town aflame. Mantis clutches her rosary beads, dodging sparks from outlets and fixtures. The other sisters cower in desperate prayer. She holds a candlestick both for illumination and defense, and when she makes her way out and into the mist, she slips and cuts her cheek on the sharp stem of a poison hemlock. The wind snuffs her flame, and after she spies her way up the brick path to the medical clinic, half of the structure has crumbled to rubble. A howling queue of civilians waits outside. Mantis falls forward onto her elbows, and the gravel makes its way into her like splinters of shaved metal. Despite the circumstance, she is affronted by the power of her own slender beauty. She curses the Lord for this matter—that she cannot match the ugliness of the scene around her, that she stands out. She is an outlier, living as contrast. Her eyebrows furl and she screams my name for help. I cannot reach her without the web, and suddenly I fear our tether has been clipped, umbilically.

I type my address into the message box, delete, type again, then finally press SEND.

Mantis does not reply, so I do the same again, hoping to see any sign of life and to give her a place to run toward. But no. There is an error message, and our chat window closes. When I attempt to reboot the program, it fails. Her username no longer exists, it tells me. Gone. Evaporation.

I pop an antacid. It lodges sideways in my throat, and I choke until my cough ejects the tablet and my spittle seeps into the carpet fibers.

In the kitchen I gargle water from the tap, then dampen a slice of white bread with milk to soothe my esophagus and to provide myself a meager amount of sustenance. A cockroach claws its way out of the electrical socket by the telephone, and I think of what people say about their ability to survive nuclear fallout, but I don't want to muse on that. I slam it, smear it across the marble surface with the edge of my fist, and rinse it down the garbage disposal.

Headlights cut through the window blinds, the dead bolt releases, and in struts Mom with a plastic bag. She's all a-giggle, happy and filled with three courses. She comes in for the hug, and I press my chin to her forehead.

"Where is he?" I say. "The King."

"In his car listening to his cassettes." She extends the bag for me to reach inside, and I remove a box of sparklers. "He wants to give us space." She sees the trail of insect. I wipe it away, and she smiles like it never happened.

Mom insists on lighting the sticks on the beach, so she wrenches her feet out of her heels, and I notice they've ballooned again, swollen from ankle to toe. She stops me when I bring up her circulation. Mom breathes heavily, and I wonder if it's tipsiness from the night out, but there is no whiff of wine. I ask if she hurts. She doesn't answer, just tugs my wrist to follow. I grab my coat.

The sand takes her up to the ankle, but me, I feel buoyant. I am lighter alongside my mother. I could float across the Gulf of Mexico if I chose to, big belly up, drawn by the Gulf Stream into the Atlantic beast and back. Mom stifles a wheeze into her elbow and tries to play it off as a laugh. Her breath has gone short. She points eastward, down the shoreline, and in the middle distance, a lonely hot air balloon glides gently home to Earth. Probably lovebirds, high on kissing and helium inhalation. Its small flame dims. They land safely from such height.

"I didn't know anyone was allowed to fly those at night," I say.

Mom looks at me with a shine in her eyes—the sort I know from her old yearbook photos, gleaming with youth and a long, fortunate future. "How about," she says, "we let everyone off the hook tonight?"

I shuffle into the ocean only because she asks me to. It's coldest around my toenails. The hem of her dress is now soaked, and I can't help but look to where her lungs are hidden, then to where her heart lives, imagining the struggling artery that connects the two.

"Your pacemaker," I say aloud, and my mouth dries from the rough texture of the word. "Does it really work?"

"It works exceptionally," she says and walks backward, barely missing a pile of tangled weeds. "Unfortunately, *exceptionally* is all it can do."

Finally we strike up our sparklers and do a little marveling at the size of the moon. I accidentally allow the stick to burn my thumb. It hurts like grieving, so I let it fall and hold the finger out to show my mother.

"What is life to you?" she says. "To you specifically."

The world has me cornered, so I say, "I don't know. An accumulation of seemingly minor moments, that, when compressed into segments, create escalating consequences, which eventually influence our collective experiential decisions on the planet, thereby causing a perpetual series of syllogistic patterns until we inevitably extinguish."

A big fish, now, swimming unusually close.

"Why don't you love yourself as much as you love me?" she says, and I am thunderstruck.

I try to conjure a response, but this only makes my memories activate, those of a single mother and her only son, infant images: bubbles in the bathtub, the surprising palms of peekaboo, birthday candles and tree ornaments, car seat buckles, the tickling of my soles. "Are you afraid you don't deserve it?" she says.

I try to breathe more deeply, from my diaphragm.

There are tears, obviously, but the ocean mist conceals them against my cheeks. Mom reaches to hold me, and I bend to press my temple to her shoulder. In a tenor, she sings the hymn I used to love from Sunday mass, "On Eagles' Wings," that windy song. I step back, eased.

She lights one last sparkler, and The King's watch shows a quarter to midnight. I remove Rex's camera from my coat pocket in order to capture a spirit all but vanished. My mother twirls. Her hair is newly short and dyed red. Before, she'd always found that color too daring. She is gaunt in face and stature, but in her current movement it is no longer jarring—an unwinding figurine in a jewelry box. I snap away. I capture grace. She poses, then steps over a blue crab and kicks the surf in my direction. Sure as hell she would swim if she could, but her heartbeat won't allow it. My mother asks me to guess the letters and words she writes in the air, her flaming, winding strokes, and I use the last click of the camera to preserve the instance. The ball will soon drop, but here, over the Gulf of Mexico, the stars remain random. They cross each other's brilliance and dance over and behind us to the mainland side—the vibrance of '99 waning.

A week before the spring equinox, year 2000, my mother died of cardiac arrest, and I try not to dwell on it too much or too little.

It occurred the night we went to the bowling alley. We both made fun of my foot size as I struggled to knot the laces of the rented shoes, and I joked that she was one to talk. My mother could barely lift the lightest ball, so I would hold her arm and help guide it backward, then forward, to push and urge toward the pins. She winked with both eyes when a few would fall. The two of us, slipping on the hard wood, clumsy as clowns in baggy clothes.

Now it is just The King and me. The King has moved into the house, into Mom's room, because he misses her. He still spends his nights in despair—crying in the living room, in the bathroom, sometimes even on the floor of *my* room when I am compelled to join. We are closer now, after many months of this year. At the end of each, he writes me a check for half the rent. I brew the coffee in the morning. In the evening he prepares supper.

Rex, the over-lover of life, stopped by to deliver his sympathies and salutations, but he wrote no card. He was cruising west to find California, he said, to pursue late-life political ambitions or maybe even a little commercial acting. I wished him well with a handshake and nothing more.

I've taken to pedaling my Schwinn to campus, but this morning I hitch a ride on the back of The King's garbage truck because he gets a kick out of it. I white-knuckle the rail and nod to all who will never experience this privilege and power. Today, though, The King doesn't drop me at the pedestrian trail. Instead, with no decal, he parks in the student lot—who is going to tow a vehicle like this?—and asks if he can sit in on my classes. He's a fish out of water in his company polo. I wear my wool suit jacket even though it's thirty-two Celsius.

At 8:50 it's Roman Mythology. The King takes a spot in the back corner, and I tell the kids he's here to evaluate the learning experience. Confused, they engage their best behavior. The King asks the student next to him for a sheet of loose-leaf and a pen. He writes when I speak.

I've grown more confident in manipulating the accoutrements of the classroom, so I use the projector to bring to life a rendering of the Roman Cerberus, a three-headed canine, the guard and minder of the underworld. A springy boy in glasses asks if this animal is indigenous only to the Mediterranean or if it has ever come to the contiguous U.S. Before I can respond, The King pipes up. "Listen, bud," he says. "It ain't real. None of this shit is actual or factual."

So as not to pierce anyone's bubble, I tell them mythology is as real as we perceive it to be. The Romans saw in these gods beauty and hope and justice and fear.

In my opinion, a figure of the past is only fictional if you let those truths fade or be forgotten.

In my office The King wants to know what the fuck that even means, and I shrug and say that in this line of work you have to think on your toes, that it's part and parcel of the gig, and that sometimes words might simply spew as such. I ask if I can see what he wrote down, and he supposes so as he tosses the folded paper across my desk. The sentimental element in me expects a romantic moment in which the sunlight splits the cloudy shawl over my window to illuminate a vulnerable poem, The King having connected the metaphorical implications of today's lesson with the sweetness of Mom's legacy. But it's not much, a crude sketch of Cerberus the dog smoking a cigar and a scribble to further look up the subject at the library.

There is an hour before my next class, but The King doesn't take the opportunity to leave. He sticks around, folds his arms over his stomach, and falls asleep with his mouth open. Rex's camera sits on my bookshelf, and no doubt its contents have overwhelmed The King, to whom I've told what's on the film: undeveloped, my mother, she lives in there.

A trait I've absorbed from The King's demeanor is the desire to console. So I stand to reach and hold his shoulder. I even wet my lips to whisper like my mother would, but the door opens with no warning.

For a moment I expect Mantis, as I do lately, often, paranoid and fearful. Now thrown into the bin along with my computer, she remains a specter, no longer needed, and I am unsure if I would even be welcoming of her arrival. Mantis was born of my past self, not of my present maturation. If I were to meet her, or whoever controlled her messaging account, I would like to say: *Thank you for the help and benevolence, but your manifestation is a stark reminder of my tendency for agoraphobia, the diabolical characteristic I am in the process of expunging.* Or something to that effect.

However this, here and now, is only a frantic student, a boy with hair to his narrow shoulders. I struggle to recall his name, and he pays no mind to the sleeping man in the chair. He's been absent this week, he says, because his dorm has flooded, he says, because his car is getting repaired, he says, and his parrot is sick. He has documentation. The boy asks for an extension. I grant it.

When my classes finish, The King is off to complete his rounds, so I get home by way of city bus. Inside the portico of our town house, against the door and nestled beside a clay pot of grayed soil, rests a delicately wrapped bouquet of calla lilies, tulips, peonies, and one rose—beautiful and tenderhearted—a gift that arrives every twelve or so days since my mother's passing, that one might reasonably conclude is, in fact, from Mantis herself. But the card is nameless.

Inside, the refrigerator drones, and a wren sings along from outside the kitchen window. The word is harmony. I clip the stems, remove any browning leaves, and lay the flowers on the dinner table for The King to arrange later.

Hounds Run

Two nights after Apollo 11 shot for the moon, my mother threw a toaster at my dad's head and called him a word I'd never heard her use before. It got him square on the ear as he walked into the kitchen, and he said something like goddamn it or here we go again. The thing didn't break, but it knocked a whole tile loose from the floor. My older sister, Dawn, wasn't home, gone to who-knows-where, so I sat alone at the dinner table, pushing some peas across my plate with the arms of my glasses. In times like these, when particularly anxious, I would often take them off.

My dad rubbed the side of his head and looked at me like I was supposed to help him.

"A teenager," my mom said. "Now it's clear who you are. You are the man who sleeps with teenagers."

"No," my dad said. "I am not that man, Pamela." The dog barked liked like she had something to say also, and my dad pushed her with his foot. "I do not sleep with teenagers," he said. "This was one. Singular. Seventeen years old. And that does make a difference."

Janette—a friend of my sister. Plainly and simply, my dad had courted her for more than a year, giving her strange gifts when she'd come over—books of what he claimed was original poetry, a hand-drawn map of Florida with red circles around every city where he owned property. She'd eaten here often. And when she did, my dad would make his spinach salad, which he said was good for vitality. She would say thank you, Albert, and he would say no thank *you* for your thankfulness. I was twelve, and even I saw it coming.

Earlier that day, while my mom and I read the paper together—*Earth is here, the moon is here, the rocket is in the middle*—Dawn came home, makeup dripping. She'd seen my father, she told us, mouth to mouth, then body to body, in his car, parked in a section of town where, believe her, no insurance salesman ever parked. She'd snapped photos—proof—with her Instamatic. And to hell with it all, Dawn told us, she was leaving this house and we'd all be lucky if she didn't come back to burn it down. Dawn went to her room, and ten minutes later she left with a duffel over her shoulder before my mom could find any words.

So now, finally, I spoke up from the dinner table. "Dad, please," I said. "Stop it."

My dad pointed at my face, but he looked at my mom. "Here we go, Pamela. See? In front of J.J. You want to do this right now, let the kid see you like this?"

"Just say you'll stop doing it," I said. "Just say you're sorry and you're wrong and that you love her and Dawn and me too, and then everything will be fine, and Dawn won't burn the house down."

"Oh my God, enough," my mom said. She stood and left for the living room, crying—sobs that drowned out Cronkite on the television.

"Christ," my dad said. "Is forgiveness too much to ask for?" He kicked again at the dog. "We've got men flying to the moon, but you want to dwell on *this*? Lecture me in my own house."

My dad ran the tap and threw water over his face. He didn't dry it with a towel. Instead he let it drip onto his shirt. He asked where the hell was Dawn, said it was time they took a drive and talked a little about how life works. But my mom lay, face buried into a sofa cushion, silent, and I had to answer for her. When I said Dawn had run away, he told me it figures and went to the garage.

It was useless to say anything to my mom—not because she wouldn't listen but because she'd fallen asleep like she always did when overwhelmed. Her body shut down, it seemed, whenever she panicked. It would move on its own, trying to guide my mom to wherever her dreams directed. She was a sleepwalker, had been for a year, and I didn't disturb her now so as not to stir up those dreams.

I cleaned my plate and gave the peas to the dog. Then with the dislodged kitchen tile, I left out the front door to meet Anya, who waited for me in orbit.

For the occasion, Anya and I had built our own lunar module in the woods. We'd stolen three lawn chairs from a neighbor's patio and draped a blue tarp over them. She was fourteen—had two years on me—and because Anya also had more muscle and height, she'd driven the edges of the tarp deep into the dirt with found railroad spikes. I tied the top to a hanging branch to create a point. Anya cut a small rectangular patch out of the side so we could see the surface, and I attached a bunch of my father's Nixon pins to the outside. After Anya told me Tricky Dick was actually an asshole, I drew wiry antennae on his head and renamed him Dick Slug. I could make her laugh, and that's why I loved her, why I lay in bed all night imagining us on a desert island for the rest of our lives.

I found Anya inside, sitting cross-legged. Her feet were naked. The shoestring headband I'd given her hung delicately over her ears, and the sequins Dawn had glued on sparkled when Anya turned to say hello. I had put the headband in her mailbox a week after we first met, a year ago, after she answered the door when my mom dragged me and Dawn to offer the new neighbors a casserole.

Since then, Anya wore the headband almost every time I saw her.

"I brought a tile," I said. "I could tape it somewhere inside, and it could be a control panel or something."

"That's a smart idea, J.J.," she said. "But any additional weight at this point could affect us during reentry. And you wouldn't want to burn up in the atmosphere, believe me."

Confident and calm, she spoke like my mother never could—with a willingness to confront a problem head-on and fix it.

"Of course," I said.

Now Anya and I lay inside the module, on the dirt, side against side. She wore a dress that looked different than usual, a green one, shorter, more floral and earth-toned, and it showed the pale skin above her knees. I grabbed her hand hard.

"We have to wait two days," she said, "to get to the moon."

After a few still moments, a yellow jacket flew straight through the cutout and into the tarp. It hovered above us, showing off its dexterity by jetting quickly to the side, then slowly up and down in some strange, rehearsed pattern. Orbital intruder, Anya called it.

I curled into a ball, sure the yellow jacket had stopped in midair to taunt me, give me a wink.

"You're a baby," Anya said. "Stop shaking."

I said that no, no I was not shaking and stood to try what I'd seen my dad do many times—flick the sucker right out of the air.

"Just leave it be," Anya said. "It's probably got a kid or two at home, and you don't want to break up a family."

I managed to get underneath it, and in one clumsy motion I hit it straight on its middle. The yellow jacket didn't fall but stammered through the air, only wounded. So I flicked it again and sent it straight down and onto Anya's neck. The stinger—I saw it—sunk into her skin, and the thing fell limp, dead and partially inside her.

"You idiot," Anya said, then tore out what she could of the insect.

"I'm sorry," I said. "I'm sorry. Don't cry."

"I'm not going to cry." She grabbed my wrist and pulled me down to her. "I'm not you." With the knuckles of her index and middle fingers, she squeezed then twisted the skin on my neck.

"It's only fair," she said. "Now suck it out."

"What?"

"The stinger," she said. "I can't really do it myself, can I?"

And no she couldn't, so I went for it. I placed my mouth around the bump, worried my lips were too dry, too wet, too small, too big. I pulled and she told me harder. So I pulled harder, and the stinger, the tiny needle, slid out of her flesh and onto my tongue.

"You guys are fucking," the older kids said as they pushed through the bottom of the tarp, six of them. I didn't know any of their names or how they knew about our module.

Anya said hell no we weren't, and J.J. would be the very last person she'd do anything like that with.

I don't know why I then swallowed the stinger. Maybe I didn't want everyone to see me spit. Maybe I wanted to preserve inside me what had been inside her.

"Where's Dawn?" a guy said to Anya. His hair was longer than my mother's. "We haven't seen her, and she has the acid."

"How would I know?" Anya said. "Why are you asking me?"

"She's lost," I said. "Or missing," I said. "Dawn's just gone, okay?"

The guy nodded toward Anya and said *she'd* know.

The older kids sat in a circle, and Anya joined them, pulling me to the ground with her. She looked at me like, some things, I don't tell you. A girl rolled a thin piece of paper around some stuff she pulled from her pocket and lit it like a cigarette. When it was passed to her, Anya took a drag. Clearly she'd done this before, with these kids, probably in here. When it passed to me, I pulled in the smoke and held it, acting as though it didn't feel like my chest was being ripped open. Then I coughed and they laughed so I said goodbye. And once out of the woods, I gagged myself. I tried to throw up what stuck in my throat.

On the walk home, I flinched every few steps—something over my shoulder, something breathing on my neck. I asked myself: If shadows had shadows, could those shadows move on their own? I thought I saw an opossum with a human face. I stayed in the middle of the road, far from any bushes, houses, or trees.

We lived in a suburb called Hounds Run, along the Gulf Coast and directly across the state from Cape Canaveral. I once asked Anya what she thought of that name, Hounds Run, and she told me it sounded either like a movie about a pack of dogs chasing you or a movie about you chasing a pack of dogs. I asked her which one she thought I'd be, chaser or runner. And she told me neither—I'd just be the one watching the movie.

I pulled open the door to my house and quickly closed it behind me. I locked it, then unlocked it, then locked it again because I was the only one who cared about keeping my mom safe, keeping her from being taken in her sleep.

In the kitchen, under the harsh light, she stood at the stove frying eggs with her eyes closed. Without saying a word, I led her to the sofa and covered her with a quilt. I wondered where her dreams would take her if she ever made it out of Hounds Run—maybe to Jupiter, Florida, to find the knife salesman who'd once left his card, or maybe to Hollywood where she said her first boyfriend had moved, maybe even to Russia to marry a Communist.

I kissed her forehead, then turned off the burner.

♦♦♦

The next day my mom joked about slicing open her eyelid, said maybe if she could never close one eye, she'd never have to completely fall asleep, and I wouldn't have to worry about her leaving. I said please don't do that, and she said of course she wouldn't, but I didn't trust her.

We walked the neighborhood, looking for Dawn—the sun so hot the street and sidewalks looked hazy, like when the television wasn't tuned correctly.

"Why does it do that?" I said.

"That's the least of my worries," my mom said.

A turtle stood in the middle of the road, clearly unsure if the time and effort to reach the other side were worth it or if he should just turn around. That summer, Anya and I had already seen four smashed by passing cars. All but one of the turtles died slowly—crushed shell, legs and tail trying their best to keep working. But one, its head slid straight off and into the weeds by the retention pond. Anya fished it out with her bare hands. The eyes remained intact, but they bulged so far out, I thought they'd pop at any second. She told me that's what *I* looked like most of the time and tossed it far into the water.

"Where exactly are we going?" I said now to my mom.

"On some sort of mission," she said.

So we knocked on doors.

The Davidsons hadn't seen her. Miss Halloway said maybe but it could have been a deer. And the doctor in the two-story said if she'd jumped the fence into his yard, the dogs would have torn her to shreds by now. My mom responded, "If you see Dawn, say she can come home. If you see her, say she doesn't have to run."

We found Anya sitting on the steps outside the front door of her house. She threw a yo-yo toward the sky, back and forth.

"Are your parents home?" my mom said.

"They're at work," Anya said.

Two cars were parked in the driveway, and it now seemed as if Anya sat guarding, hiding something inside.

I peered into the door's window, and her family's Soviet flag still hung on the living room wall—red, yellow, hammer and sickle. I'd never been inside and never met her parents. But the flag I'd seen many times, when she'd opened the door only enough to fit her body through. I often worried Anya would get caught with it, get taken to some room with gray walls and no mirrors. But Anya said it'd be fine. She was an astronaut, not a cosmonaut. Her parents liked the colors better, was all.

"Well, have you seen her," my mom said, "my Dawn?"

The mark on Anya's neck had turned redder—a purple outline now around the sting.

"No, ma'am," Anya said. "Maybe she ran away."

To get inside the house, I asked if I could have a glass of water. Anya looked toward the door and said, "Um, sure," and I thought about how if love might be knowing secrets, knowing secrets might take some prying. But instead of inviting us in, she went inside and returned with a glass for me and my mother. So I said I needed to use the restroom.

"The toilet's not working," Anya said. "The water."

"But you just gave us a drink."

Anya shrugged and bent to tie one shoe, then the other—dirty white sneakers, multicolored laces. They were my sister's.

"After that," she said, "it just then stopped working."

I looked to my mom to see if she'd noticed the shoes. She stared down into her glass. She studied the water and the flecks of dust that floated on top.

Together, at the same time, she and I found Dawn.

Anya gave me an a-okay, meaning we'd meet later, and I hesitated before giving her one back.

My mom and I sat in plastic chairs on our patio. The pool water was stagnant and green, covered in a layer of mosquitos, ants, and the corpses of a few water-bloated frogs. The summer before, when the water was still clean and chlorinated, we had an Independence Day party out here—my parents' friends, clients of my father, cousins and family I'd never met who somehow knew I struggled with my fractions. And Janette. She had just been passing by, my dad said. And she should stay for a bit, my dad said. After swimming, when Janette stepped out of the blue water, wearing what older girls wear when they step out of blue water, my dad motioned to her. He had a towel.

That night, my mom walked in her sleep for the first time. She tried to leave the house barefoot, wearing her church dress and pearls, but I stopped her before she could get the door unlocked.

Whenever I'd tried to clean the pool since, my parents made me put the net away. There wouldn't be another party, and they seemed happy to watch the water mold over.

"Dawn will come home soon," I said. "All of her records are here."

"Maybe she will," my mom said. She crossed then uncrossed her legs.

"Why didn't you tell Anya that you noticed Dawn's shoes?"

"God knows," she said. "Why didn't you?"

I removed my glasses and folded in the arms. "God knows," I said.

Five sandhill cranes flew in from the west, giant things, and slowly descended, growing larger until they landed in our backyard. One opened its beak and gently closed it around another's neck. The smallest spread its wings wide in order to demonstrate its right to be among the group. Stupid birds, I thought. I'd seen one of them choke to death on a live snake.

"Do you think there's something like them on the moon?" I said.

"Does it matter if there is?" My mom bit at the nail of her index finger.

"I think so."

"Maybe people who walk in their sleep are space aliens," she said. "Maybe I finally need to leave for the mother ship."

I told her to please not do that, and as we heard my dad park in the driveway, she said she was only joking. Of course she wouldn't.

The cranes flew off to invade someone else.

That night Anya arrived in a brown dress, shorter than I'd seen before. She breathed heavily and said it was only because she sprinted the whole way. The sweat on her face seemed different, though—not thick or runny but applied, like makeup. She was glossy of Dawn.

Anya peered through the rectangular cut in the tarp and into the darkness.

"I can see it now," she said. "The moon. The great night-light. We will arrive before the next nightfall if this module stays intact."

Anya retrieved my kitchen tile from the dirt and typed some mathematical predictions on its surface.

"The big cheese," I said.

She picked up the phone, an old shoe, and said we should call Houston to tell them we were on course, but I said wait, don't. I didn't care at all about Houston in that moment.

"Anya," I said and placed my fingers awkwardly on her back. "Do you think, tonight, that maybe we could do what Dawn's friends thought we were doing?"

The words were hard to say, and out of fear I might have said them too timidly, I repeated them. My throat felt like chalk.

"You mean fuck," she said. "You want us to fuck."

"Yes," I said. "Like I could put my hand on your leg or something. And you could touch me back. Maybe."

She squinted through the tarp as if she saw something blocking our path.

"Well, J.J., that would be groovy," she said, using a word I hated. "But I don't think Michael Collins, Buzz Aldrin, and Neil Armstrong are fucking each other right now."

And Anya was right again, and I was embarrassed again, and there was silence again until I finally said it because I had to. "Dawn is in your house," I said. "And I want to know why."

She turned to me as if she had been anticipating this, and she held my arms to my sides so I couldn't mess with my glasses. "Think about how it feels when you hold my hand," she said. "Think about it really, really hard." Anya then placed her lips on the bridge of my nose, and my skin went flush. "That's how it feels when Dawn kisses me, okay?"

If I had been attacked by a million yellow jackets then, it wouldn't have mattered in the least.

"So what do you think?" Anya released her grip and bent down to reach again for the shoe.

"Call Houston," I said.

And she did. She put on her deepest voice and faked the sound of static. Everything was fine, Anya told them, as if nothing of any consequence had happened at all.

We both stood, unsure of what to do or say next, and instead of lying on the floor and talking about inertia, trajectory, or if that Russian dog would ever make it home from space, Anya said she should leave.

"But I'll see you tomorrow," she said. "Your house. For the landing."

"Groovy," I said.

After she left, I feared that this module wouldn't stay on course at all, that it would float right past the moon and eventually land on some unknown planet where there were no Anyas and they only let you eat cat food.

Outside, I pulled and pulled but couldn't tear the tarp from its branch. All that fell was a pine cone. I squeezed it until my palm hurt, and when I threw it against a tree, it bounced back and hit me on the chest.

In the driveway, my dad waited with the top down and said, "Get in." We sat for a while, alone together, until he started the ignition and slowly backed into the street.

"Where's Mom?" I said. "Is she here?"

The car stammered forward.

"Guess what?" he said. "I kicked the bathroom door in."

"Are we looking for her?" I said.

"She was just standing there, J.J., not even looking in the mirror," he said. "She was facing the window. And it was open."

"Is she still there?" I grabbed the sleeve of my father's shirt. The wheel jerked a bit to the right before my dad corrected it. "Where are we going?"

"Facing the window, J.J.," he said. We slowed while passing a green-painted house, and my dad stuck his head out to look for a moment before speeding up again. "Pointing a damn steak knife. Right at her own face."

She had done it. She had cut her eyelid open. She had hurt herself, probably bleeding, probably crying, now, on the bathroom floor with no one to help but the dog because no one had been there to stop her because no one had ever listened.

"No," my dad said, as if I had spoken aloud or as if he could hear my thoughts. And maybe I had, or maybe he could. "I took it from her," he said, "and she just thanked me."

"And then she ran?"

"Yes," he said.

"Why didn't you chase her?"

"I was waiting for you."

"Was she asleep?"

"I don't know," he said. "I can't tell anymore."

We turned down Oak Bend, the street where all the dentists lived, and the moon was now ahead of us, a small waxing crescent—I'd memorized the phases. I removed my glasses, and in the sliver of light, I swear I could see a crater on the surface. On one side stood the same five sandhill cranes, flapping their wings, reaching with their beaks. On the other stood Anya and Dawn, looking down at me, mouthing words I couldn't hear.

"Hello," I whispered. "I see you."

The car slowed again. "Keep your glasses on," my dad said. "Or how are you going to find her? How are you ever going to find anything?"

On this street, all the neighbors' children had strung wires from streetlight to streetlight and hung giant American flags between each. Every flag was attached by its top, so they ran parallel to the ground and, in this way, created a long row of waving red, white, and blue—a procession that took you to the end, to the cul-de-sac, where one of the banners faced you directly, and you had no choice but to admire it for what it was. And what it was to almost everyone in Hounds Run, everyone in the country, was a luminous pride and a naive but hopeful anticipation of what would come next, after tomorrow, when something that seemed impossibly far away, the moon, would now be touchable.

On our way back up the street, as my dad braked to turn onto the main drag, we saw my mom. "She's dead," I told my dad, and he said no, she was just tangled up in a dentist's bushes.

I opened the door and ran for her. She had fallen backward into a row of hedges. Her eyes looked like she'd never blinked in her life. I got on my knees and crawled in, positioned myself exactly like her.

"Are you awake?" I said.

"I have the same question."

She asked me to slap her, so I aimed for her cheek and palmed her.

"Well why'd you do it so quick and easy?" She smiled. "My own child."

"I want you to be awake."

"Yes," my mom said.

My dad made his way over and raised his finger to yell, but when his mouth opened no sound came out.

My mom asked if he had anything to say.

"This is the part where you finally tell her something, Dad," I said.

He offered his hand, but my mom wouldn't accept it.

To my right, in the street, what could have been a moccasin from the lake, or what could have only been a tree branch, stretched itself from a storm drain and cast a shadow from the light of the moon. The shadow curled and twisted its way toward the three of us. I thought it might strike.

My dad said, "So what do you think of me, Pamela? Am I the man who sleeps with teenagers? Yes, I am. You said it. Is this excusable? No. Not by you. Not by God himself. Why did I do it? I don't know. I probably won't ever know, won't ever have an answer for it until I'm groveling outside the pearly gates. Do you have an answer for why you sleepwalk? I bet you haven't got the slightest damn clue. And you know what else is shameful about me? I used to laugh about it. I used to laugh until my eyes were wet as all hell. And Janette. Both of us would just die laughing. 'Last night Pamela tried to trim the shag carpet with the push mower,' I'd tell her. 'Last night Pamela tried to put the dog in the oven.' 'Last night Pamela pissed on the fucking floor.'"

"Shut up," I said. "Shut up. I'll punch you."

"But you know what I did yesterday? I felt sorry. I came home early, with a present. Flowers. To make amends so we can at least get back to pretending we're a family. You two weren't there, neither of you, so I actually tried it out. I tried to walk, blind, like you. I tried to connect, tried to *understand*. I closed my eyes and walked the house. I started at the sofa. And I did it well enough, Pamela. I didn't think it was all that hard. I poured myself a glass of water. I was able to feed the dog. But then I found the glass doors and went out on the patio. And this is what happened, and you can go ahead and laugh if you want. I walked right into it. Right into that retched-up swimming pool. And then, well, I didn't feel like I should feel sorry anymore. I woke the hell up. Like *you* should. I took a long shower, and I drove my guilty ass right back to work like an adult does. Be an adult, Pamela. Do your job. Wake up."

I looked, and there was no more snake, no more branch. There might never have been.

"It's one thing to be blind," she said. "But it's a completely different thing to be unconscious." My mom stood and wiped the dirt and pine needles off her sides. "I guess you won't ever get it," she said. "But it's all right, Albert. At least we can say you tried."

The afternoon Apollo 11 landed on the moon, my mom told me to pack a bag so we could leave for Aunt Rachael's in the morning. I asked about Dawn, but she said don't worry about it. Now Dawn could look for *us*.

I cracked open my bedroom door, and from inside, I watched my mom and dad. They sat on the couch staring at the television, the dog lying between them. Without looking, my dad reached to pet its neck and accidentally touched my mom's hand. He pulled back quickly and cleared his throat out of embarrassment. I wanted my mom to scream, punch, get revenge for all the damage he had done her. But she didn't.

"We've got men trying to land on the moon, and you're worried about *us*?" my mom said to my dad. "This, whatever it is, is fine now."

"Because it's over," my dad said.

"Because it's over," my mom said.

I lay on the bed and put a pillow over my face. I thought this might be a good time to cry, but I couldn't force any tears. I heard the front door open and close, then the giggling of Anya and Dawn. Eventually my dad yelled something about the future, history, mankind, and for me to get my ass out there, so I did.

My sister and Anya sat cross-legged and just to the side of the screen, their fingers interlocked. No one said a thing about it. I was amazed.

We all knew each other as best we could.

Now that I'd be leaving Hounds Run, I wondered if Dawn would be coming along. But that was a concern for the morning. I pushed the dog off the sofa to sit between my parents, and Cronkite finally shut his hole. My mom took a deep breath, her eyes wider than I'd ever seen. The telephone rang but no one answered, and my dad even muttered the Pledge under his breath.

Finally, we saw it.

After it all, the module itself rested securely, safely, on the eastern shore of The Sea of Tranquility.

Anya turned to me and put a hand over her mouth to muffle the sound. "We landed, commander?"

We had never discussed rank because I always assumed Anya to be in charge. But now, for the first time, she'd granted me a title.

I made the same gesture back. "By God," I said. "I think we did."

Rag and Bone

After hustling 300 at nine-ball and nearly having my ear sliced off in the bathroom, I'm thrown onto the street. I can barely walk, and I'm shaking even though it's summer. I find the one working pay phone left in Tampa and call my dad collect while a man in an Army jacket laughs at me from across Seventh Avenue. I am embarrassed for being so skinny.

It's three in the morning and there's no answer, so I take the cord and wrap it around my throat. I pull tight but tell myself to knock it the fuck off, call again. This time he picks up. We breathe in sync until I tell him what happened.

He says he loves it, says he fell asleep thinking of types of trouble I could get into, played out scenarios over in his head: me screaming while pressed over the front of a patrol car, me puking in a holding cell then being told to lick it up. Soothing as counting sheep, is what Dad says.

He finally gets here, and on the way home he hands me the rubber tourniquet from under his seat, and I wrap it tight to find a vein. Dad hums over the radio. It's his favorite song.

◆◆◆

Three nights later, I'm heaving into the kitchen sink when Dad gets home from his PTSD therapist and dares me to go out and do it all again. He dangles a dime bag of the powder over my head, then slides it into his shirt pocket. I'd rather peel off my own skin, but I say okay, it's my pleasure, same bar, same game. Dad smiles and gives me an envelope. Inside are five twenties and a pamphlet for the Marines.

Your choice, he tells me. Entertain him. Or enlist.

I walk out the front door, and the dead bolt locks into place. I remove the brochure. A kid in fatigues—looks my age—smiles at me, invites me. Call the recruiter and it could all stop, this game, this trap.

I take a bite out of the Marine's face, chew, swallow, then throw the rest into the bushes.

On the bus, I stuff my fingers into my own shirt pocket, searching, feeling for a bag that isn't there but might appear like magic to heal me. A woman three rows ahead asks am I okay, is there anyone she can call, and why am I screaming bloody murder. I didn't realize I was. Now she's looking me over, and I get so mad at how bony my elbows are that I turn from her and push my face against the window.

A pit bull chases us along Powhatan for a while. He jumps over potholes, dodges trash. Tongue flapping and teeth grinning, he's having fun, so much goddamn fun. And for one flash of a moment I am too, until we hang a right onto Sligh and the dumb thing keeps running straight.

At my stop I get up to leave, and when I pass the woman, she tries to hand me a rosary, says she's got plenty and the gas station on Twelfth will let me take a shower for free. I stop, stalled there, and stand until the driver yells for me to get off, and once outside, I find her window and tap on the glass. The woman looks down at me and waves. I mouth any random words, so she'll always wonder what I tried to tell her.

It's not raining, but the air is hot and sticky. There's sweat behind my ears. I want to drink all the water in the world, so I go inside and order a glass at the bar. I think about Dad at home alone, rubbing lotion over the POW tattoo on his chest, over his two bullet scars. I picture him picturing *me*. I'm crouched in the desert. I'm aiming a rifle. He says attaboy, son, attaboy!

I ask a man who looks like a cartoon sailor if he shoots pool, and he agrees to a game for twenty bucks. I miss every pocket by three or four millimeters on purpose. I shake his hand congratulations, and he calls me rag-and-bone man, I guess because I'm so thin. A rag-and-bone man is someone who used to roam around during the Plague, steal other people's trash, and then sell that shit just to get by, day to day to day. I know this. I dropped out, but I've read the textbook.

Now I say we should play for sixty, and he says I'll eat lead if I'm a hustler. I've heard much better. He places his bills next to mine on the edge of the table, gives me a wink. I win before he even gets to lift his cue—a stupid move. Too obvious, too eager. I reach for the cash, but he the jabs the end of his stick into my Adam's apple, and my legs give out.

There's yelling from the bartender, and the cartoon sailor drags me to the parking lot and smashes my face against the back of his Astro van. I close my eyes and try to enjoy the pain for whatever rush it is. Sometimes it can feel good, like when you bite your own tongue.

When he's done with me, he throws me onto the cement, takes my envelope, and preaches something from above like he's a tough guy or a prophet. I give him a thumbs up and mumble God, Guns, and Country because that's what I see on his bumper sticker.

I lie for a while, then stand and walk east until I come across a group of women in front of a hotel and show them my open forehead. The women are as young as I am, and their dresses look too nice for this part of town. One lets me use her cellphone to call an ambulance, but

I call Dad instead. When I finish telling him about the cartoon sailor and the beating, he asks if that's all. He's disappointed. I make up something, anything—like I stole a car, like I wrapped it around a streetlight, like the cops picked me up and put their cigarettes out on my neck. He knows I'm lying. I beg him to let me sleep at home. I ask for mercy. But I know the drill: not impressed, not tonight. I say I love him, but he hangs up.

The nice woman reaches into her purse for something she might use against me, so I gently hand her phone back and tell the whole group, all of them, that I will pray for them, I swear, if only they would just pray for me too.

It's close to one in the morning. Jim Berry and I are sitting on the steps of his trailer while his girlfriend and baby boy sleep inside. I know Jim Berry from the bar, back when I tried to shake him for fifty bucks and he took pity on me by playing dumb. Now he throws me oxys when I'm too sick to breathe. During the day, he picks strawberries out in Pasco County. He's offered to get me a job there, but I never have the time. Picking and picking, he tells me, all day picking. I call him Jim Berry because he's from Guatemala and won't give up his real name, even though I tell him everything about me. He looks around fifty or something, but who knows.

Jim Berry does me a solid and gives me five of the things, but this is all he can spare for the rest of the month. I take off my shoe, and on the step below me, I crush the pills into dust and shape it into as clean a line as I can muster right now. Jim Berry just watches in silence, and after I snort the stuff and put my head in my hands, he waits with me until I'm breathing more easily and my right eyelid stops twitching.

I tell him thank you. Jesus, thank you. And he asks how long I'm going to keep letting my dad fuck with me.

Thing is, Dad's not fucking with me. My dad loves me. Or he will. He just wants what's best, wants me to protect and serve like he did, wants me to suffer until I agree. My dad is a man of noble causes, and this is what I tell Jim Berry. He doesn't buy it though, says we both know my dad hooked me on smack to sit at home with his dick in his hand thinking about my funeral.

I'm about to say, *Okay*, I'll just cave then, Jim Berry, I'll just enlist, go to war for my dad's affection like some sort of Ancient Greek statue or dry-cleaned good old boy, but a tiny kid, couldn't be older than eight, walks by, drinking out of a two-liter of Sprite.

Jim Berry yells at the kid to get the hell home to his abuela and to take it easy with the sugar. The kid keeps walking and says his abuela hasn't been home in two days. Jim Berry says of course she hasn't, and he doesn't look surprised.

I start nodding off, so I ask Jim Berry for a bed and maybe a sandwich. But he tells me no, it's time to leave now, I'm not his family. And of course, yes, he's correct.

So I actually end up taking that shower at the gas station on Twelfth. The woman on the bus was right. The night clerk just gives me a key to the bathroom out back without asking any questions. I turn the knob all the way right, freezing cold, and sit in the water with my clothes on. Even through my shirt, I can count my ribs.

I imagine Jim Berry, all tanked-topped and pony-tailed, pulling my head against his stomach, holding it there and rubbing it like he probably does his baby's. He asks whose country I'd be fighting for, exactly. His? My dad's? My own? What about the kid wandering alone with a soda bottle? Our battles are individual, one on one. I don't know, Jim Berry. I don't know. And I fall asleep to the rhythm of his breathing, unable to answer.

I wake up wet, congested, and sick. On the floor is a rusted drain. I think of dragging my wrist across it, just to see if the option's still there, but realize I've never wanted that way out. I turn off the water but still feel dry inside.

In the gas station, there's a long line that must be the morning commuters, but the clock says three in the afternoon. Everyone gives me an odd look because I'm trailing water everywhere and, I guess, crying. But I can't really turn that off anymore. Some tall guy wearing a golf shirt asks if I need any help, and I just say ha ha, swimming pool, got pushed in. I grab a Gatorade from the fridge in the back, as if electrolytes will help any of this, and leave the store. What are they going to do, stop me?

Dad's truck isn't here, but the spare key's on top of the mat, so thank God he's shown enough sympathy to let me in today. I go through his bathroom drawers, where he keeps his pills, all prescribed by his therapist at the VA: Lamictal, Ambien, Seroquel, Valium, Lexapro, Viagra, Edecrin, and so many goddamn vitamins. I empty the bottles onto the floor and look for any opiates he may have hidden. Nothing. Still, a lot of power in these pills. I could swallow one of each and see what happens. I could swallow them all and black out. But right now, I just need to stave off the withdrawals and the gagging, the sweat, the cruel illusion of dying.

A dog barks. Dad whistles. I pick as many of the things off the tile as I can and throw them back into the drawer. Dad calls my name because he knows I'm here and I'll come needing a fix, needing affection.

He's in the living room, on the couch, and wants to show me something. This big son of a bitch, a mastiff, rolls all over him and pins him to the cushions. Dad's got his tongue out, licking this dog more than the dog licks him. A giant red, white, and blue handkerchief tied around the dog's neck, its muscles are so defined they have veins the size of ropes. Dad tells me the VA gave it to him, even let him name it. Uncle Sam, Dad says to me, Uncle Sammy. Man's best friend and all that shit.

I'm so jealous I want to tear the dog's skin off and chew the meat from his skeleton. I want to take his head and force it through the sliding glass door. I want to stab a syringe into the corner of his eye, make him dependent on *me*.

I scream at Dad, scream that I am Rag-and-Bone Man. I am Rag-and-Bone Man come to serve him.

He pours Uncle Sam a bowl of kibble, even throws some cheese on top, then tells me to hold the leash while we walk him. I'm white as a ghost, Dad tells me, and I say I wonder why as I'm pulled by the dog.

And of course it's uncontrollable. Dad laughs while the dog rips my arm to the right, left, forward. I say Dad please, I can't, but when my shoulder cracks and my vision blurs, I fall to the ground and get dragged across the lawn. Dad says if I don't learn how to walk dogs, dogs will always walk me, then finally takes hold of the leash so I can let go.

I run inside. I put some ice in a pillowcase and tie it around my arm and shoulder. When Dad comes in, red faced and giddy, he goes into his bedroom, and I hear the clicks of the iron safe. I yell to my dad that I can be good, that I can do better, and he tosses me a shoebox with all the junk I need for now. He tells me I better fucking prove it and calls for Uncle Sammy.

So I do to myself what I need to do. Then I roll my neck around slowly to make it crack. The swirls and pastel colors of the kitchen floor are so light and delicate they seem painted on by an angel's hand.

All of this is how I find myself crouched behind Jim Berry's AC unit, in the middle of the night, holding a combat knife. Even though there's no rain, heavy clouds block the moon from lighting the sky.

I don't plan to hurt the baby. I don't even plan to take it. The art is crafting the *appearance* of the act. I need Jim Berry to catch me. And if the only guy who knows me, the only person even close to being a friend, kills me, crushes my head and smears the brains across his carpet, all the better and so be it. I move to the window—pitch black inside—and pry it up an inch. An odor, whatever they ate for dinner, lingers. The television is turned off. I get angry at how little more I have to slide open the window to fit my thin body through, and it's hard with one arm immobile in a makeshift sling.

Jim Berry's stash sits in plain sight, just bottles and bottles on the kitchen table. I pocket as many pills as I can and swallow at least seven or eight. I know where the baby sleeps—in his own room, in his crib. I hesitate though.

Again, always, I'm thirsty. I can't see anything at all in the kitchen, but I feel for the sink so I can drink quietly out of the tap. And when I do, it tastes better than good. It tastes how I imagine the waters under a frozen stream taste.

I pull my shoes off so I can silently move toward the baby's room, and as I leave the kitchen, I notice a pan left on the stove with meat gone moldy and green. The oven has been left on. I turn it off.

The door to the baby's room is cracked open, and small plastic stars glow from the far wall. The hinges don't squeak at all, but when I move forward, my foot touches something, someone's leg, and I almost yell. Jim Berry's girlfriend sleeps in front of the doorway, and her boyfriend is curled into her side. I don't know who I stepped on, but no one says a thing.

I suppose this is fine. I will move behind the crib, and when I tug the baby's ear he will scream, and Jim Berry will hopefully grab my knife and plunge it into me until I am half dead, maybe remove a finger or even a whole limb. And I will crawl to my dad's feet.

So I reach for the baby, but as I do, I notice its hair—black like Jim Berry's and in contrast to the white skin from his mother. I rub my finger along his hairline and whisper good boy, good boy.

Jim Berry coughs and rolls onto his back, his chest lifting and falling rapidly. I stand tall and stretch my spine. It cracks with pain. His girlfriend inhales a breath for so long I don't know how she isn't inflating in size. I hold the knife over the baby, and I think of rosaries and pool cues and heaping mounds of dog food, and here it goes.

Through the pain of my shoulder, I move my right hand toward the baby's face and poke his puffy cheek. A small bubble grows then bursts between his lips. He coughs and slowly opens his eyes. He looks directly through me before he screams like he's damning me to hell. But Jim Berry doesn't wake up, and neither does his girlfriend, so I go over and tell him that hey, I'm going to kill your baby. No response. I kick him in his side, and he moans.

Then I understand the obvious.

I bend over and pull back Jim Berry's eyelids, and his pupils are rolled into his skull. He's so high he's lost in space, and the same with his girlfriend. The baby's still screaming but in short bursts. The kid's saying something different to me now, telling me that, sure, he can see how I live, but take a look at *his* world.

I kick Jim Berry's foot out of the way and go to the kitchen to find a bottle. I look in the cabinets, slamming them shut when I find nothing. I finally pull one out of the goddamn trash, but it's broken in two and the nipple is missing. In the fridge is a carton of milk only a few days expired, so I carry it back to Jim Berry's baby boy. Holding the container with my hurt arm, I dab the finger from my other hand into the liquid. I place the milk on the baby's lips, and finally it quiets down. I wet my finger again and do the same, and he smiles, this baby. He's even giggling. Again and again I bring the milk to his mouth. I don't know why, honestly—I've never done this kind of thing—but I bend over and kind of kiss his forehead. His lashes flutter.

Eventually Jim Berry mumbles something coherent, and I know I have seconds. So yeah, of course I think about stealing the baby. We could roll as sidekicks, escape, grow fat, get high only on gallons and gallons of milk. But instead I do something else. I place the carton on the floor and exit the room, leaving Jim Berry's son to the unimaginable circumstances he may find himself in every single day.

I ask God and God answers. Jim Berry's kid might find a way out or he might not. But I am damn well nobody's protector.

I walk for hours until I find that old pay phone, and when I do, it looks even dirtier than before. I pick up the receiver and dial my dad's number, but after it rings once, I hang up. I poke the sides of my face, press into my sunken cheeks. I run my fingers down my forearm, stopping at my wrist to check for a pulse.

I lift the phone again. This time I try a number I've memorized but have never used, one scribbled onto a legal pad in Dad's sock drawer. It belongs to my mother's home. The house sits against the beach, on the bay, where she and my sisters play Scrabble and give high fives.

A woman answers, but she has a foreign accent. She says she doesn't know my name, I have the wrong number, no one with those names lives there, she's sorry.

The man in the Army jacket stands across the street again, determined, fists raised to the sky.

I walk out from the stand, pulling the cord taut, and I say one more thing to the woman on the other end:

I believe you. But can I see for myself.

Guilt and Matter

He cries and vomits. It starts with a foamy leak down his T-shirt, followed soon after by a stream of guts and color. He is embarrassed. This is a good thing, I think. Still, I wonder if it's an act rehearsed for these moments. He has been making the rounds to apologize to my family members. I light a cigarette and offer him one so that he can say what he came here to say and get it over with.

We are sitting on my porch in Tampa. This is the summer. It is too hot for this.

"I killed her," he says, "but I don't feel like a murderer."

"If you are a Catholic you can ask for forgiveness," I say. "Otherwise, I don't know what to tell you, and it's not my job to absolve you."

He is a bald man, much older than me, with a bulbous stomach barely contained by a God is Good T-shirt. I wonder if he wears this shirt often. Maybe he was wearing it when he didn't look left, when he pulled out onto a dry, clay road, forcing my cousin's car sideways and into a cement culvert. She died when her neck snapped.

He didn't look left.

As the man talks I don't listen because I don't care what he says. He will never matter.

I think of the cruel dice game of the Fates: my cousin driving home from a weekend-long college orientation. She was probably happy, probably a little hungover, and it was her birthday. Eighteen years old.

She got to spend all of one day as an adult, and now her casket rests in an aboveground mausoleum, stacked on top of other enclosed bones—a giant filing cabinet waiting for a spiteful God to one day slide it open and finger through.

If I believe in a God, I don't want to.

"She's in a better place," I hear the man say. "I just know she is."

I worry that this may not be true, that there is no better place than here, all of us trapped within our individual circumstances, riding out our small segments of chronology until we reach the witching hour.

I worry that this is it for us, as it is for her, that my cousin in her dust-bin afterlife will never get to feel whatever it is her accidental killer gets to feel, right now, as he tries to repent.

Still, I know the man didn't mean it.

He is innocent.

I get him a rag to clean up his mess.

Lucia

The first time I married Lucia, we were in the fifth grade. The date had been set a week earlier, after I sneaked her a silver ring I stole from my mother's jewelry box. Lucia thanked me, and I said I loved her, and she said, yes, she loved me too, as long I didn't sit near Bethany Dickerson during lunch anymore. It was a deal.

So we stood there during recess, under the sycamore tree at St. Theresa's, with the entire class gathered around. Mikey T. presided as always, due to him being the nephew of Father Patrick, the principal, and having the deepest voice any of us had ever heard come from a kid our age.

These weddings were common at St. Theresa's and happened the same way, at the same place, about three times a month. Sister Gale pretended not to notice, smoking her cigarette in the corner along the chain link fence. Tommy chirped notes from his recorder.

Lucia and I locked eyes, hers still red and swollen from crying that morning. Her mom was in trouble, she'd said, for real this time. I had told her to stop worrying so much. This was more important. The best day of our lives.

But Lucia had not told me—because I was too selfish to let her—that her mother had begun a morning ritual that would continue for almost two weeks. Lucia now awoke to her mother painting more quickly and furiously, as if in a rush, on canvases. Her mother had started cooking fried eggs, toast, and sour jam. Her mother allowed Lucia an extra cup of sweet coffee. And whenever Lucia would grab her backpack to leave, her mother would pull Lucia's face against her chest and, through tears, say, "Probably goodbye soon, mi vida. Probably goodbye soon. Be safe. Promise. Don't ever stay where you don't want to be."

Unaware, I held her hands, felt the sweat between our palms, and took in the honey smell of the sycamore.

"Do you, Lucia Estrada," Mikey T. said, "take this servant of God as your husband, to hold and to kiss?"

The kids whistled, laughed, howled. Mikey T. hushed them and said to respect the reverence of the sacrament.

Lucia attended the school off a Diocesan scholarship. She lived in a trailer and got most of her food from the government. My mom made an extra bagged lunch for me to bring Lucia each day, and the other kids knew but acted like they didn't. No one messed with Lucia. They were intimidated. Lucia was the smartest student in our grade, wasn't scared to chew gum in class, and could shoot a three better than all the boys. To them, she was a mystery.

Lucia said yes, and I said the same, and we gave the whole group what they wanted. A kiss, the first—the actual feeling of contact, the dampness. It's something that stays with you, of course. But this isn't to be romantic. Lucia's kiss wasn't so simple—not a snapshot of innocence. It was complex, dense, as much a singular moment of bliss as it was a life sentence. Something you relive in random moments, whether you want to or not—when your shower water turns cold or when you could swear you heard the doorbell ring or when, on the sidewalk, you accidentally break through the clasped hands of a young couple.

The other kids got three rounds of dodgeball in before the bell rang, but I didn't join. Lucia said she wanted a few minutes alone to talk to Sister Gale, and from across the yard I watched them both make the sign of the cross. Sister embraced Lucia the way I wanted to, and they closed their eyes, trembling in prayer.

Every day, my dad drove Lucia to and from school because she lived alone with her mom and they didn't own a car. Her trailer was in a park that sat along the beach, but Lucia stayed away from the water and everything that lived in it. I told her once not to be scared of the jellyfish and stingrays, said they probably liked her just as much as I did, and she told me to shut the hell up and she'd never been afraid of anything in her life.

On the drive one afternoon, we sat in the backseat, leaving plenty of empty space between us so my dad wouldn't suspect anything. We rode with the top down, and I waited for the moment when the air would begin to taste salty—the miserable indication I wouldn't see Lucia until the next morning. Lucia kept the ring I gave her in the pocket of her plaid skirt.

"Math tests," my dad said over the wind. "How'd they go?"

I said I did okay, but Lucia didn't answer, distracted by a long, yellow school bus that drove alongside our car. Younger children smashed their faces against the windows, pulled open their cheeks, pointed their frightening, curled tongues at us. I nudged Lucia.

"Oh," she said. "Test was easy. Didn't need to study."

"Great," my dad said, looking back through the rear-view. "You should start studying, though. It gets harder."

The bus stopped at the side of the road, and we left it behind. Lucia and I watched the children pour out like marbles.

"Maybe," Lucia said.

After we entered the trailer park and turned the corner around the For Rent signs and the manager's office, my dad slowed to a stop as Lucia's home came into view. A police cruiser, lights off, sat in her driveway. An officer stood against the hood, nodding as a woman in a suit scribbled on a notepad.

My dad told us to stay put, please, and everything would be okay. He left us to go find answers.

"They caught her again," Lucia said. "She told me they would soon, and she was right, and I should have been here, and I should have stopped them because I could have stopped them."

"Your mom?"

"Yes, my mom." Lucia tugged her hair downward in a closed fist.

"Selling those things again?" I said.

The woman in the suit showed my dad the papers, and he pointed, asked questions, before pausing and slowly wiping sweat from his forehead.

"Those *pills*," Lucia said. "You don't know anything."

I slid closer to her, but when the adults walked toward us, zombie-like, Lucia opened the door and ran. She was headed for a cluster of palm trees, the trail that led to the beach. I followed, and my dad yelled my name, and the cop yelled my dad's name, and I yelled Lucia's.

I caught up to her on the bridge that crossed the marsh, and I begged to know why she kept running. Lucia stopped to look at me, like prey would a predator, then kicked off her shoes and continued, leaving desperate footprints in the sand.

Once, Lucia told me an old man with no arms or legs lived inside the shed behind the rocks, though she had never seen him or even tried to. Her mother called the place a haven, and the man was someone who would tell Lucia what to do, where to go, if she ever found herself in need of escape. I knew he didn't exist. Still, I was jealous.

Run to me, Lucia.

While she tried to pry the shed door open, I grabbed her by the collar. She fell sideways onto a sharp rock that cut through her polo, and a small red streak leaked from her side and through the fabric.

Lucia grabbed my waist and twisted me to the ground. She straddled me and cocked her fist to swing, but the cop caught her arm. He lifted her. He tied her wrists together with a strip of plastic like she was a criminal. My dad finally reached us, but he was out of breath and said nothing.

"Why would you stop me?" Lucia said to me.

"I'm sorry," I said.

We marched up the beach and to her trailer, and once there, Lucia told me she hated me. She hoped I'd die, and if I didn't die soon, she'd kill me herself.

The woman in the suit waited with her legs crossed, heels dug into the dirt. She told the officer to cut Lucia free. He did, and the woman led Lucia into the mobile home. They talked for a while, Lucia and the woman. My dad and I stayed back but close enough to see them through the window screen.

"Her mom's been arrested, if you're wondering," my dad said. "I don't feel bad for the mother. But how can you not feel bad for that innocent child?" He spoke as if talking to himself.

"Where are they taking Lucia?" I said.

"I have the same question," he said.

Next to the rear wheel of my dad's car, the ring I stole from my mom and gave to Lucia poked halfway through the dirt. The sun, almost to setting, shone onto the silver, and the light reflected a narrow beam straight at the siding of Lucia's trailer. My dad picked a lovebug off my shoulder and tore it in half.

Over the next three months, Lucia was brought to my house for a few days at a time—first a weekend, then the majority of the school week. We didn't talk at all until finally, after my parents forced us to finish an entire game of Monopoly as a unit, Lucia threw her cash into the air after winning. "You're dumb as shit," she told me. "Dumb as a literal piece of shit."

"Language, please," my mom said.

Once adoption papers were signed, Lucia moved in permanently, and we shared the same last name.

For Lucia's sixteenth birthday, my dad rented a boat and took us out into the Gulf. I was allowed to bring a friend of mine, a girl named Roxy with pink hair and spike earrings. She'd turned me on to Alice in Chains. They were all right.

We all wore swimsuits except for Lucia, who had on a T-shirt, jeans, and a tightly secured life jacket. Whenever the boat caught a wave, she grabbed my mother's arm and said we were downright idiots about to sink and drown.

Roxy leaned over the edge with a fishing pole, and Lucia asked her what it felt like to be a murderer.

"You don't like fish anyway," I said. "What do you care?"

"I care about morals," Lucia said. "Unlike Roxy the fisher girl."

Roxy reeled in her line and laid the pole on the boat's floor. "You're right," she said to Lucia. "I'm *so* sorry."

"I know I'm right."

"Lucia, please," my mom said.

My dad pointed east and told us to check this out—dolphins. Five of them, they glided together, circling the boat, synchronized in their leaps and twirls. Roxy pulled my arms around her waist and said it was a pretty dope sight, romantic. Lucia watched but stayed crouched to keep her balance.

"You know these monsters have sharp enough teeth to rip both your arms off if they wanted to," she said. "Plus, they have violent, painful sex for fun."

Roxy kissed my cheek, and I turned to see Lucia mimic a gag.

When the sun set, my dad docked into the marina and moored the boat to the landing. He removed Lucia's birthday cake from a cooler and burnt his thumb while lighting the single candle in the center. He told us to sing. Lucia said God no, no thank you, but we all began anyway. I could tell Lucia enjoyed the moment, somewhat, even though her gaze stayed fixed on Roxy, who eventually turned away frightened. A gull swept from the sky and hovered inches above the water, flying against the current, toward the horizon, and chasing the last red bit of the sun. I don't think it was the lighting. Lucia looked content to be with us. And at the end of the song, she clapped.

"Blow out the candle," my dad said.

Lucia said we all knew she didn't believe in wishes. Because if they were real, her mom would be here singing also, but look, she isn't, so watch this. Lucia closed her hand around the flame, and it went dead. A tiny trail of smoke rose then disappeared in the air.

"But thank you for today," she said. She shook my parents' hands. "I mean it."

Sometimes it seemed her eyes blinked like, I might be trapped.

We arrived home and found Roxy's older brother sitting in his pickup. A metal band was playing downtown, and we were late. My parents had agreed as long as Lucia and I didn't start wearing mohawks or forming militias to fight the Man. I'd told them that's punk, not metal, but when they asked for the difference I said I didn't really know.

"Get in," the brother said, then dropped a lit cigarette from his car window onto my parents' driveway. He started the engine and pointed at me and Roxy. "You two in the back. Lucia up front."

My dad snuffed the butt out with his boating loafer, picked the thing off the ground, and threw it into the recycling bin.

"Good God," my mom said.

Roxy and her brother went to Gaither High, by the Chinese buffet where Lucia and I washed dishes. Lucia had only met the brother once, at a party I dragged her to, where he showed off his amplifiers, said he loved Latina chicks, and pinched her ass. Lucia only came along now because she could defend herself and because she knew I wanted her near me. We stayed together. That's just how it worked. I sat in the truck bed, cross-legged with Roxy on my lap, bouncing with every bump in the road.

"We are *so* in love," Roxy said, and I said sure.

"Promise?"

The pressure from the rusty metal under my legs hurt so badly I'd have said anything.

"Absolutely."

"What about Lucia?" she said.

Through the cab window, I saw Lucia twirling her hair, nodding in response to Roxy's brother.

"You're crazy," I said. "She's my sister." I kissed the back of Roxy's neck, but she pulled away for a moment.

"Is she really though?"

The band was awful, but Roxy loved them. She took swigs of passed-around whiskey and traded endearing middle fingers with the crowd around us. She whipped her hair onto my face, and I tried my best to look like I belonged. I swung my arms, pumped my fists to the bass drum. Eventually, Roxy moved away and a guy in dreadlocks—looked twenty-something—shoved his tongue down her throat. I grabbed one of the passing bottles and threw back the last of it. From behind, Lucia ripped it from my hands, placed it on the ground, and motioned for the exit.

Lucia covered her hand with her shirt sleeve to open the door, and in the parking lot, I asked what happened with Roxy's brother. Lucia told me not to worry about it, don't ask. I said that was okay with me.

A possum squeezed itself out from under a dumpster, carrying a shard of glass in its bloody mouth.

"Let's walk home," she said and kicked at the loose gravel on the pavement.

"That would take like two hours," I said.

"Good," she said and grabbed my arm to wrap it around her shoulders. She was cold.

In October of that year, Lucia sat down for Sunday breakfast wearing a sleeveless dress. She had straightened her hair and done her nails. It was as if she became ten years older than me overnight. My mom poured her a glass of orange juice and said she looked nice, particularly motherly.

"Thank you," Lucia said. "But I'm going more for daughterly."

Her mother had been moved to a halfway house and, that day, could take a free hour at nine-thirty. Across from the townhome on Fifty-Sixth Street, Lucia would meet her mom at the Burger King, mother and child connecting for the first time in over five years.

I'd asked Lucia why she never visited the prison. Lucia didn't want to see her mom in a uniform. Why no letters, phone calls? Forgot her Spanish. I never asked much else. I chose not to think about her mother. I chose not to believe that Lucia was trying to break free.

My mom poured syrup onto Lucia's pancakes, and Lucia said thank you but she wasn't that hungry.

"You need a full stomach today, Sweetie."

Lucia bit her bottom lip. "I told you I don't want anything."

My mom straightened her back, and my dad peered cautiously over his newspaper. "All right then," my mom said and began the blessing. She asked the Dear Lord for good health, fewer thunderstorms, and better poll numbers for H.W. Also, she thanked God for Lucia's meeting, for the glorious gift of granting forgiveness to Lucia's mother.

"And what exactly did she do wrong?" Lucia said. "I don't think she very much needs God's forgiveness. Or yours."

My mom looked at my dad for help, but he only shrugged. "Honey," she said to Lucia, "your mother sold drugs to people. She sold lots of drugs to lots of people. That is very dangerous. You know that."

"I consider it work," Lucia said. "Have you ever worked? Do you even know what work is?"

My dad got up and ran the tap to wash his plate.

"I didn't think so. Yes, my mom sold drugs. But she also sold her paintings. People have the right to drugs and paintings if they want them, don't you think? My mom was providing a service. So she could provide for me."

My dad dropped a dish into the sink—ceramic against steel—and apologized.

"And just because you all want me here doesn't mean I have to. Remember that."

She told me to meet her outside in fifteen and walked out the front door, slamming it behind her.

"She's just nervous," I said.

My mom slid Lucia's pancakes to me, said the keys were on the counter and I needed to fill the tank on the way back.

Outside, Lucia was writing on the sidewalk with a piece of chalk left over from the neighbors' kids. When I called her name, she startled, threw the chalk into the grass, and wiped her hands clean, careful not to let the dust touch her outfit.

Lucia didn't say a word to me on the way. She bit her nails, tugged on her hair. She scanned the radio stations before settling on AM talk radio—Clinton this, Bush that.

"Since when do you care about the election?" I asked.

"Oh," she said. "Is that what they're talking about?"

I parked in the back of the lot, and Lucia touched up her lipstick in the visor mirror. I was to wait in the car.

"This means a lot, thank you," she said. "Just knowing you're close by." I kissed her cheek, and she left, stepping carefully and straightening the sides of her dress.

I took the car through the drive-thru, ordered a milkshake, and tried to pay attention to the radio. A talk show host explained the importance of Clinton's saxophone. It helped public perception, he said, the hip factor. True, I guess. Tommy from St. Theresa's now played sax in a ska band, and he was pretty cool.

After forty-seven minutes, Lucia tugged on the door handle, and I let her in. She gleamed, absolutely glowed. When she put her hair back up, she seemed my age again, and I was happy.

"She only has 'til next February," Lucia said. "Well, technically, two years in that house, but if she stays clean, they'll let her out in February." She took my milkshake from the cupholder and licked the chocolate off the straw. "Then she'll get her trailer back. After six years and seventy-two days, *we* will get our trailer back."

I drove out of the parking lot and didn't bother to ask Lucia where her mom was. The woman could have still been inside. She could have already walked to the halfway house. Or she might not have ever been in the restaurant at all—as mythical as the old man with no arms or legs, who still waited for Lucia, lonely, in the shed.

At home, Lucia skipped into the house, but I stayed outside for a moment. The sprinkler heads spun, throwing water onto Lucia's chalk letters, making them blurry but still legible. *No vuelvo*, they read.

Lucia wasn't coming back.

At three in the morning after senior prom, I found Lucia in the backyard crying and ripping handfuls of grass from the ground. I was still a little messed up, but I'd run out of booze and the weed was wearing off. I chewed a hard mint as if that would hide anything, and it burnt the hell out of my tongue and throat.

"So he touched you," I said. "Just like that?"

"Don't," Lucia said. "Don't you dare."

I stayed my distance, about ten feet, but had to lean against one of the tree's ancient branches for stability. What must have been a million crickets all joined in chorus to produce one static sound—the world's largest audience.

Lucia had been angry I'd skipped out on the dance. But it's not like we could have asked my parents to take pictures of us as dates. Like always, we would have had to act like brother and sister despite the jeers and suspicions—no hand-holding, no dancing—having to kiss or make contact only outside or in an empty classroom. So instead I met with the guys from the baseball team, carved an apple into a pipe, and smoked myself silly all the way to Roxy's house party, where we waited for the oversexed and eager prom-goers to show up. Lucia arrived and changed from her dress, held around the waist by some kid with a goatee and nose ring. I spent the rest of the party carving her name into a bathroom wall.

"He didn't touch me," she said. "Forget it. Nothing happened, you asshole."

"Well that's not what I heard. Not what Mark said. Not what Ralph said. Not Liz or Monica. Do I need to keep listing? I have a long, long list."

Lucia threw one of her heels, not at me but toward a tattered Bush-Quayle sign nailed into the fence. "I didn't let him, okay. He didn't ask. He just did it. Simple as that."

"In Roxy's house?"

"In Roxy's bedroom," she said. "You've been gone all night to God knows where, and if you'd have come for me, he wouldn't have touched me like that, and you wouldn't be so pathetic right now trying to make me feel sorry for *you*."

I cupped my palm over my right ear but found it made the crickets louder. They were taunting me, laughing at me for having failed at something that meant so much.

I sat next to her but didn't have a smoke, so I took out my lighter, flipped the lid open and closed and open and closed just to watch the wick burn. After a while, Lucia plucked a single blade of grass, reached over, and held it in the flame.

"Mom's going back to the penitentiary, you know," Lucia said. "In Tallahassee. Caught her selling right out of that halfway house."

"Why didn't you tell me?" I said. February had passed. The two years were almost up.

"Because I'm embarrassed I didn't see it coming. Embarrassed for ever having hope for anything or anyone."

"Maybe she was doing it for you," I said, pathetic and blatantly disingenuous. "Saving up."

"Maybe one day I'll tell myself that," Lucia said.

Over the years, I'd grown used to how we communicated. It had been the same since we were small kids. Avoid the point. Get angry. Wait for that empty space in a conversation when the mind goes blank and bodies connect.

I made a move, but this time Lucia laughed at me, just stood and towered above me. I thought she might spit at my face. And it was an awful laugh, one that sounded like everything in her life had lost meaning, stopped making sense. Like everything was now a joke. Hilarious.

"You are an idiot," she said. "You don't understand anything."

The crickets went silent, as if it had grown too late even for them, or as if Lucia had scared them away.

"It's not your fault he touched me," Lucia said. "But I have the right to blame anyone I want to for it. I have the right to give myself a reason, even if it's not true, even if it's unfair. So I blame you, and you can either accept it out of love for me or not."

She turned to leave, but I stopped her.

"I accept it," I said.

"Okay then," she said.

At the end of the summer, I took a job for the city stringing wires, and Lucia left for college. I visited once every two weeks and didn't ask what she did when I wasn't there, and she didn't ask the same of me. After four years, I begged her to come home, then drove up with a truck ready to pack her things.

"Well," she said, "looks like I'm still stuck with you."

I laughed at the joke, but she didn't.

The second time I married Lucia, we had to show we weren't blood related. Skin color wasn't enough. Our kid wasn't enough. It took a blood test to prove it. In the clinic lobby, a nurse held our daughter, Cynthia, while Lucia and I were stuck with needles. I winced. Lucia didn't blink at all because I'd bet that she would, and she promised to prove me wrong.

It felt strange when they called a few days later to confirm what we already knew: that no matter how attached to Lucia I felt, there would always exist a disconnect between us—even through marriage—that we were untethered and could be pulled apart at any moment, each of us remaining, at least chemically, separate.

I drew a picture of two strands of DNA on the back of a pharmacy receipt and handed it to Lucia while she nursed the baby. One strand had a face, arms, top hat, and cane—the other a ponytail and basketball. She told me that they weren't called strands, idiot, that they were polynucleotides. She taught biology at a college downtown.

She asked me, "Does this child have any of my features at all? Does she even look like she should be my kid?" And I told her yes—the nose, the eyes, certainly the smile.

"No," Lucia said and lifted Cynthia away from her chest. "She looks exactly like your mother. She could be your mother's own kid."

After quitting changing diapers altogether, Lucia had recently stopped even burping the baby, so she handed Cynthia over to me and left to use the restroom. I found myself, frequently then, having to apologize to the child in whispers. "Your mother loves you, Cynthia. Somewhere in there, I promise, she does."

And Lucia did love Cynthia. I am allowed to be sure of this, sure she was only too scared of mothering, too damaged from her own.

Now we stood in the chapel at St. Theresa's, where we once went to school. Newly ordained Father Mike Tomlin presided, and in the crowd sat only a few people: my parents, Cynthia, two aunts, one uncle, and no one with Lucia's blood. An organ played. We kissed. People cried. A kid in a white robe poured wine into cups on the altar.

That's all.

My parents agreed to keep the baby for a week, and the next night, after we drove out of Florida, we stayed in a rundown motel because Lucia never wasted money, even though we had enough. A large woman at the desk told Lucia it was a hundred, and Lucia said the sign said sixty, and the woman said well now it was a hundred, so I just gave the woman my card.

Lucia played with the window unit, trying endlessly to set a certain temperature. We had sex blandly, monotonously—nothing new or special. Afterward, she took so much time in the shower I fell asleep, and we never got to the wine.

For what felt like days, I dreamed of a pale man with such a long reach he had to roll his arms up like hoses just to walk around without dragging everyone into his embrace. And when I woke, Lucia had left a note behind and the window unit at full blast.

I unfolded the paper. *No vuelvo*, again, is what it read.

I haven't mentioned many of the good times because that's not so much what this is about. But there were plenty. Memorable times, beautiful ones.

Here:

Lucia running a string out the window of my room and into hers, tugging whenever she wanted to talk.

Lucia and me chasing cranes out of the backyard.

Lucia, my parents, and me laid out on a blanket by the pond.

Lucia lying, telling my dad we'd never kissed.

Lucia worried that he already knew.

Lucia teaching my mom how to fry plantains.

Lucia on my back as we walked into the lake so she could finally learn to swim.

Lucia swearing never to swim again.

Lucia's dancing, the rhythm of the music on her cassettes.

Lucia buying a year's worth of film so we could take one Polaroid together every day.

Lucia yelling at me for smoking a cigarette.

Lucia kissing away the taste.

Lucia and me in the backseat of the station wagon.

Lucia and me in our friend's closet.

Lucia and me in an empty church.

Lucia and me against her dorm room wall.

Lucia's face while we watched a meteor shower from the top of the airport parking lot.

Lucia's wave to me as she walked across the stage with her diploma.

Lucia knocking on a marble countertop and saying this, now *this*, is the house.

Lucia rubbing menthol gel on my feet when I got the flu.

Lucia snoring.

Lucia praying.

Lucia.

But when pieced together, fragments don't always make a whole. And facts don't always tell the truth. Of course I searched for Lucia, but only for a short while, until I remembered what I'd learned in the beginning. You simply do not chase Lucia. My mother says that she must have been seeing a different man, that she'd fooled me all along. But that's not it at all. She was in search of freedom, a new life as told by her and no one else. I had tied her to me, kept her in a life she never felt she completely owned. Lucia left because she had to. For better or for worse, she had to rewrite it all from the beginning.

Knowing this, it hurts less every day. I understand more than I don't.

Today, I'm taking Cynthia to see the shed for the first time. She's old enough, and at five she wants answers I can't give with words. Lucia and I kept up the shed over the years because she felt it was her duty. Eventually my dad fortified it with beams and insulation. I now own the land it sits on but have never met the man with no arms or legs.

The trailer park is now a Salvation Army, so I take an access road that snakes around and crosses through the marsh. I point to an alligator, and Cynthia's eyes grow wide with excitement. It's winter, so when I stop the car, I wrap her in a coat but remove her shoes to walk through the sand. I tell her to look at the waves, then the horizon. That's where the world curls. If you run enough that way, you'll either fall off or, maybe one day, end up right back in this spot.

I race Cynthia to the shed. After I open the door, I flick on the Christmas lights Lucia ran around the ceiling's edges. On one wall the Polaroids stretch from top to bottom, side to side. All of them. Exactly 366. A leap year.

I feel Lucia's kiss, smell it, taste it, the first one under the sycamore, as I always do when I come in here. God knows, we were married until we weren't, and sometimes that's enough.

On the opposite wall hangs a framed portrait of Lucia at about Cynthia's age, painted by Lucia's mother. The shadowing is perfect, the contrast smooth. The brushstrokes are dramatic but not enough to appear inauthentic. And the facial features capture a girl exactly as I met her, smiling wide and determined.

I walk Cynthia around the inside of the shed. I let her run her small fingers across everything so maybe she'll understand it all by feel and touch.

I ask Cynthia what she thinks, and she scrunches in her nose, lifts her head to deliver an answer.

"I think," Cynthia says, "that she looks like me."

A harsh clap of thunder causes her to hug my leg. I pick Cynthia up, press her cheek to mine, and wait for the rain to pass, like it always does.

Show Hands

In fact, Gilfinder can only explain the feeling in these abstract terms:

One day, he allowed his husband to freeze into a block of ice. Still warm, guilty, Gilfinder watched his husband melt and seep into the dirt forever. And Gilfinder cannot adjust to reality.

Now in his classroom, as Gilfinder writes some long division on the board for his fifth-grade class, a strange child walks in with a pistol. The kid's wearing a black ball cap with sunglasses that cover most of his face, and he reeks of fertilizer. They're stunned, Gilfinder and his students. They don't move at first. This kid just stands in the doorway and slowly lifts the gun, points it at Gilfinder's face. The tip is orange. A toy.

"Wait," Gilfinder says.

"Bang," the kid says.

Gilfinder drops to the floor. So do his children. He crawls under his desk and covers the wound between his eyes. There's only a dry hole. Not one drop of blood.

If you were to look into this hole, you'd see that Gilfinder's head is filled with many things—history, equations, wars, resolution, lust, heartbreak, jubilance, indifference, decades of baseball statistics. He is old, seventy-two, and unlike his late husband, he doesn't pretend he isn't. He accepts it, he thinks, more than most others his age. The way he carries himself makes it seem as if he is someone who has practiced being an old man his entire life. Gilfinder's the guy who says, "Well, I've seen it all." But right now, Gilfinder realizes he hasn't. He has never seen this. He has never been shot in the face.

The children are screaming, and this makes Gilfinder do the same. Over the top of the desk, he sees the kid aiming the toy at the students. Sean, then Maggie, then Geoff.

"Bang," the kid says. "Pop. Bang."

Ralph, who sits in the back and never says a word, runs toward the kid and slams him against the wall, but the shooter gets free and escapes out and down the hall. The sirens are turned on. An indecipherable voice says something through the static of the PA.

"We are shot," the children who are shot say from the floor. "We are dead. Why didn't you protect us?"

"I don't know," Gilfinder says. "What could I do?"

"Many of our parents and elders agree," they say. "You should have your own toy, for our sake."

The children who have not been shot exit the classroom one by one while Gilfinder remains under his desk, using his fingers to examine the hole in his head. He doesn't try to stop them. He doesn't say he's sorry for having been such a failure.

Eventually the principal arrives and finds Gilfinder still hiding. The building, she tells him, was evacuated over an hour ago.

"Oh poor things," she says and points to Sean, then Maggie, then Geoff. "The new kid has killed those students."

"We weren't in any way prepared for it," they say.

Everyone wags their finger at Gilfinder.

"I will go home then," he says.

On his way through the hallway, Gilfinder stops at the pottery room, where young Mr. Patchett teaches his ceramics classes with such innocent sensuality. The children love Mr. Patchett. It's hard for anyone not to. New blood. Inside, Gilfinder finds a wet mound of clay and forces the substance into the opening between his eyes. He smooths the surface with a spackling knife so no one will notice the hole in his head.

The elementary school sits among the coastal residences of the city, and as he drives over the bridge that crosses a small inlet, Gilfinder can see the Sarasota pier stretching out over the Gulf. He contemplates going there now—warning the out-of-towners about the shooter, ordering them to leave and never come back, not because he doesn't want them there but because it's his duty as a citizen.

Instead, Gilfinder cowers. He crosses through the clean, protective boundary of condos, restaurants, and securely gated subdivisions to the flea market on the opposite side of town, a strip mall now, really. All ages congregate here, smoke whatever they smoke openly because no one cares about this place anymore, especially the police. The building is pastel red and yellow, not out of choice but because the colors have faded from the sun. Gilfinder knows this because he remembers. Years ago, this was an antique shop. Almost every piece of furniture in his house was purchased here, carefully inspected for scratches or blemishes by his husband, who took his time, running his hand over every crevice, knob, and curve. Gilfinder would watch the hour hand drag itself around his watch face, and his husband would tell him to stop complaining. Always though, after lugging home the chests of drawers, bed frames, bookcases, ottomans, Gilfinder would dust them off and admit that, yes, the pieces served the house spectacularly well. Less than a week after his husband trickled into the soil, Gilfinder sold the furniture away, everything, and bought himself only a used leather recliner and a thin mattress.

He parks his car in a far corner of the lot and doesn't remove his jacket or tie. As he walks, two people say hey there buddy and get in his way for cash. They blow smoke onto his face. Gilfinder submits and hands over three bills.

Inside, past the vendors selling Tampa cigars, glass pipes, old cassettes, and vinyls, he finds the table he's looking for, and a man with a goatee and a jean jacket asks Gilfinder what he needs and says cash only.

"You have any toy guns?" Gilfinder says.

Yo-yos. Trading cards. Action figures. Video games. All lined up, unpackaged and dusty.

"Just for safety," Gilfinder says.

The man with a goatee says sure he's got guns and pulls out three Monopoly boxes from a shelf in the back, places them on the counter, and opens them. "Big. Medium. Small," he says. "You can pick 'em up. Just, please, don't point any in my direction."

Gilfinder runs his hand down the barrel of the largest one. It's matte black and plastic, but he doesn't choose this weapon. Instead, he grabs a small one, silver and aluminum, orange-tipped—the type used this morning. He is aroused. It has been months. More.

"If you like the small ones," the man with the goatee says, "I've got lots. This one even has a chamber you can pop out and spin, like this. Fun."

The man says something about political correctness, cowboys and Indians, but Gilfinder isn't listening. The pistol intimidates and thrills him at the same time. Sure, killing is killing, Gilfinder thinks. Murder is murder. But this is for defense. And when you really boil it down, really get down to it, isn't all killing protection? This is what Gilfinder wants. Just the power, for once, to protect.

"No," Gilfinder says, holding the gun with two hands at a slight angle to inspect its shine. "This'll do."

"Five dollars, and I can't go less."

Gilfinder says sure, whatever, throws his last ten on the table, and leaves without taking any change except for a greasy Buffalo nickel. He firmly presses the face of the coin into the clay between his eyes and peels it away, leaving behind the impression of the beast, an animal of courage, before dropping the nickel to the floor.

Gilfinder lifts his jacket and slides the gun into the space between his belt and pants. Maybe it's the way he carries himself now, but no one outside bothers him for anything.

He stops for milk. The cat needs it and so does he. There are four people, total, in the convenience store—Gilfinder, the clerk, and two punks with tattoos and skateboards. The lighting is fluorescent, harsh. It's hotter than outside. He grabs a half gallon and holds it by the handle with his left hand.

Gilfinder moves to the back by the freezer and studies all movement—the teenagers' sarcastic gestures and laughs as one tosses the other a bag of chips, the exhausted expressions of the cashier, whose shirt is wrinkled and untucked. Gilfinder squints, and they are slow-moving, seemingly unaware of his presence at all.

The punks open their bags in plain sight. They eat, pour crumbs into their mouths, onto the floor. He feels he should protect but cannot accurately gauge the degree to which he should defend the store, an honest business, owned by an honest family. And quite frankly, the clerk herself is complicit. She is not taking the required action to secure the inventory.

Not yet, he actually believes, has the pistol corrupted him.

He removes the pistol and holds it barrel-down, at his side. If he waits long enough, the cashier will leave the register, maybe to check the coffee pots or wipe the syrup by the soda machine. Gilfinder needs her to do this because of the button under the counter that calls the police. At least that's what he's seen on television.

The thrill in his body grows so electric that the milk and pistol shake in his grip, the world be damned. He tilts his face to the floor but keeps his eyes up, trained on all three. And sure enough, the cashier leaves her station and heads for the hot food.

"This milk," Gilfinder says, moving toward the exit.

"Sir?" the cashier says.

"This milk," Gilfinder says. "I'm taking it home, and I'm not paying for it. If you allow this, you will regret it."

They all take a minute and look at one another, confused, before the teenagers laugh again.

"Whole milk's on sale today," the cashier says and grabs the tongs to mess with the hotdogs.

So Gilfinder lifts the gun and aims at the cashier. "I'm taking the milk, and I'm not paying for it."

As he hoped, the cashier and the teenagers raise their arms. "Predictably this weapon has gone to your head," they say. "You have developed a wrongful perception of power."

And bang, pop, bang, Gilfinder fires. They fall to the floor. The cashier's leg twitches.

"None of us prefers this," they say now, dead.

Gilfinder secures his pistol, leaves with his milk, and drives home satisfied, wondering if anything is quantifiable in a world newly flipped upside-down. And, if so, what exactly does *x* equal today.

In his house, the cat has clawed the hell out of the recliner again, so Gilfinder knows he will have to sew it up. But tonight he's too tired. He nukes a TV meal and lets the cat have a few bites of the mashed potatoes. Even in the chair, Gilfinder leaves on his jacket and tie. The pistol, he lets it poke into his leg to feel its reality.

When he's finished, he throws the plastic container into the trash, on top of the other identical containers. Gilfinder hasn't cooked one real meal since his husband melted, and he dwells on this when he opens the can, every time he takes the bag out and down to the curb. His husband would be ashamed, would yell at him. His husband would be right in doing so. His husband would slap him gently on the shoulder the same way he had since they met in the dormitory decades and generations ago. Gilfinder wouldn't hit back. Instead they would smile and hug around waists like lovers do. His husband would cook him something, a proper meal. His husband cooked well. His husband cooked dishes Gilfinder could never pronounce. He cooked colorful, rich things, using spices and flavors somehow mixed with an alchemy honed over a lifetime. They would have a Scotch and a smoke on the porch. Good for the heart, his husband would say. And damn good for the soul, Gilfinder would say, and they would love each other, deeply, in many unspoken ways as well.

But when these memories come on most strongly, Gilfinder finds himself staring at the hanging shirts in his husband's closet, like he does now, and is forced to recall the stroke and the ambulance, the tubes and wires, Gilfinder driving his husband home and, shamefully, viewing his husband in the simplest of fractions, as two different people: the one who could move an arm and leg and the one frozen and solid as ice, and Gilfinder describes it as ice because that's what it felt like, coldness, and there's just no other word to use, and cold skin means death, or at least something similar, so when his husband's other half went cold too, Gilfinder swears, right now to God, that he still loved his husband the same but just couldn't handle feeding his husband through a straw in the side of his mouth, forcing puree past his husband's teeth, down his throat, and there was no other choice—it's the truth—that his husband *had* to go to a home, and that was frankly that, but Gilfinder could only visit so often because of his schedule at the school, parent-teacher meetings, etcetera, so as a consequence Gilfinder could not stop the nurse, that name-tagged Melanie Waters, from going outside for that slim menthol while Gilfinder's husband sucked for air, convulsing until he wasn't, and his husband soon lay colder, even, than any sort of ice, before melting slowly, that then-puddled tile, and this guilt crushes Gilfinder, has crushed him ever since, and now he feels like he is in his classroom but being written onto his own chalkboard with child fingers, reduced to the smallest fraction of himself, the farthest decimal.

And on and on, this is what Gilfinder thinks.

A rhythm against the front door. Gilfinder opens it to find the same kid who shot up his classroom that morning, and they both draw quickly.

They are so close. The orange tips of their weapons almost touch.

"Gilfinder," the kid says.

He wears the same hat and glasses but now smells so rancid that Gilfinder has to suppress a gag.

"How do you know where I live?" Gilfinder says.

"I followed you."

"No you didn't. You're too young to drive."

Attracted by the light, one mosquito, then two, then three enter the apartment and land on Gilfinder's outstretched forearm. They bite him, and they take their time.

"What do you want from me?" Gilfinder says, but he already knows the answer.

"But you already know the answer," the kid says.

The final mosquito leaves Gilfinder's skin, taking with it some of Gilfinder's blood, before doing the same to the kid.

"The gun," Gilfinder says.

"Of course," the kid says.

"Well you can't have it."

"I know," the kid says. "That's why we're standing like this."

"I suppose so," Gilfinder says.

It begins to rain only because, Gilfinder acknowledges, in this type of situation it *should* rain. It's only appropriate. It's as he would imagine.

The kid is soaked but remains perfectly still. Gilfinder is dry behind the threshold.

"Why do you want it?" Gilfinder says.

"Because you have it and they don't want you to have it."

"Who doesn't want me to have it?"

"The ones who are dead," the kid says.

Gilfinder tightens his grip. "Why?" he says. "It's for protection." The humidity isn't good for Gilfinder's joints, and the pain in his elbow grows almost too much to handle.

"Because more was expected of you," the kid says. "And now they are scared and angry."

With these words, Gilfinder holds in a breath before letting it out slowly.

And, "Bang," Gilfinder says.

The kid falls like all the rest.

"See?" the dead kid says.

Gilfinder secures the gun, shuts the door, and slowly walks to the closet for a needle and thread. With all his strength, he rips a piece of fabric from the sleeve of his husband's peacoat to patch the hole in his recliner. Once Gilfinder finishes, he places the instruments back into the container so the cat won't get ahold of them. He sits to feel the warmth but can't think of the meaning, can't parse out the significance of the day. He places his palm on his forehead to check his temperature, then notices the imprint of the nickel is gone. There is no buffalo. Gilfinder pushes inward, but the clay is now actual skin and skull. He uses the nail of his index finger to scratch, then carve into his bullet wound, but instead he cuts through his flesh, drawing blood.

The chair squeaks when Gilfinder pushes backward. He pushes again. It makes the same sound. If he could, he would fix this tomorrow, but he understands he will have to pay for what he has done today. They will find the bodies, and since you cannot commit homicide and simultaneously be an elementary school teacher, he will no longer be an elementary school teacher. His classroom is the only thing he will miss. And he will miss it tremendously. Of course, the children will want someone new, better, younger, and much, much warmer anyway.

Gilfinder calls the cat's name, and from across the room she turns her head toward him, yawning, clearly knowing what's going to happen.

"Watch this," he says. Gilfinder lifts the pistol from his belt and presses the orange tip into his temple. "Bang."

The gun only clicks because the gun is only a toy. Gilfinder doesn't die. There is no pain. Gilfinder should have expected, ever since his purchase, that this is how it would go. The equation was already equal. It was equaled the day his husband perished. In his hand, the pistol either freezes or burns, but at this degree of intensity, Gilfinder can't tell the difference.

"Bang, pop, bang," he says as he tries again.

Flan of the Year

Beth came home, trophy raised after finally winning Flan of the Year, only for her husband Marty to tell her to be quiet. Nixon was on the television. Well isn't this a thing, she thought. This is quite a thing.

"Honey," he said, "what do I ask for when Nixon is on the television?"

Beth lowered her prize. She swallowed.

"To remain quiet and let you be," she said. She placed the trophy on the wall shelf, next to the ceramic frame that contained a portrait of her late and beloved Weimaraner, Skipper, a noble dog who had lived in this trailer for nearly as long as she and Marty. He would have been so thrilled, Skipper. The hours, the years he had spent splayed out next to the oven, intently watching the process, examining the ingredients: eggs, condensed milk, a whole cup of sugar kept in the refrigerator for two-and-a-half days.

Now though, to win, Beth had developed a secret, an illicit addition to the strictly prescribed ingredients: the tiniest bit of melted cinnamon, just enough to fool the tongue but not enough to recognize the taste. Poor Skipper, she thought. He'd be proud.

Marty had knowledge of the secret only because he'd walked into the kitchen after Beth had pulled the drapes closed and lit the scented candles. "Are you trying to have a séance?" he had said. "If so, well, I'll leave you to it, madam."

She explained herself, her fear of anyone peering in from the outside. Yes, she felt guilty but so exhilarated at the same time. Of course Marty didn't care much about this or her flan or her cheating. But others surely would. If the contestants in the trailer park were to discover the cinnamon, well, it might be an even larger scandal than this played-out Watergate business.

"He is actually saying this," Marty now said from the couch. "He won't release his private tapes. It's 'the simple truth,' he says. What exactly does that mean? If 'simple truth' means obvious lie, then he's right. You admit it's your own guys, but you still say 'simple truth' like you're not the biggest bag of crumbs on the planet. It takes gumption, I guess, to be that much of a rat bastard."

Beth poured herself a celebratory glass of Scotch from the living room cart because why not, and she sat next to her husband. "I don't think he deserves all the criticism," she said. "I mean, we're all bastards, aren't we? We all have little secrets."

He didn't even look at her, just put his elbows on his knees and leaned forward.

"Beth, half the time I have no idea what you are talking about."

Beth threw back the Scotch. "I actually did it, you know. I won Flan of the Year. Is that something you understand?"

"Again," Marty said, "what do I ask for when Nixon is on the television?"

The telephone rang, so Beth answered it quickly and stretched the cord as far as she could down the hallway. It was Susan, calling to again congratulate her flan. "As soon as I saw it, I knew I had no chance," Susan said.

"Didn't even need to taste it first to know it. Now, really, how exactly *did* you do it?"

Beth waited a few moments to speak.

"Susan, this is why I never had children with him. They'd have either grown up to be news junkies or window snoopers by now. And frankly, I don't even know if there's a difference."

"Oh," Susan said, "this is about Marty."

"Yes, this about Marty. It's always about Marty lately."

"Has he gone to a doctor yet?" Susan said. "You know, to check things out?"

Beth paused again and decided to wait until the subject changed.

"Well then." Susan said. "I wonder what the papers will have to say tomorrow about the president. Really, this whole thing is starting to stink."

And with that, Beth wished Susan the best of luck with her flan for next year, returned to the living room, and placed the phone back on the wall. The television had been turned off. Marty shook his head, chin buried into his chest.

"I've told you before," Beth said. "But Susan is two-faced." Susan lived three trailers over, smoked long menthols, and had lizard-thick skin from falling asleep at the pool every day. When Beth used to pass with Skipper, Susan would always over-compliment, in that ominous, intrusive way that leads one to mistrust and fear but, at the same time, confide: "You look twenty years younger in that dress." "You have such evocative eyebrows." "If I were a man," Susan had said once around Christmas, after a couple of eggnogs, "I'd be all over you."

Marty lit a cigarette, but after taking just one drag, he coughed up a half dollar-sized wad of phlegm onto the carpet. Quickly, he tried to cover it with his handkerchief, but he couldn't manage to bend toward the floor. Beth didn't like this. She did not like this at all. She placed her hand on his shoulder and said it would be all right, then got up for the rag and soap she'd been using more and more frequently in these situations. When she came back, Marty was still coughing, violent sounds, a ripping of cardboard. Then it just stopped, like that.

"You know, the thing about Susan is she's lonely," Marty said. "Her grandson is crushed up from the war. No one visits. So she wants to be your friend. Big deal. You'd probably like her. Cut her some slack, Beth. For once, have a friend."

"I like her fine," Beth said from the floor. She had to scrub with vigor. It was amazing just how quickly mucus hardened and just how jaded you could become by it. "She's just always examining me." The carpet was now as clean as she could get it. But Beth knew there would be more of this, and it would get worse. She knew Marty would never agree to have an honest conversation about it. He would refuse again to see a doctor. And she knew he would never understand how much this hurt her.

Marty struggled to rise from the couch and walked toward the bedroom. He stopped when he noticed the trophy, then picked it up and turned it a few times in his hand.

"It's only aluminum," Beth said. "It's an old baseball trophy. But that thing has been around for a very long time, and I am actually the twelfth person to win it. It's quite a thing."

Marty placed it back on the shelf and arranged it exactly the way it had been before. Beth felt proud.

"So the cinnamon actually did the trick?" he said.

"Yes," she said.

The next morning the paper did, in fact, have something to say about the president: NIXON DENIES ROLE IN COVER-UP, ADMITS ABUSE BY SUBORDINATES. She couldn't read anything other than headlines now. The other words were meaningless drivel, bloated sentences with too many words. Get to the point and move on. And it is quite a thing, Beth thought, to crucify a man for having faults. She felt bad for him, Nixon, just an old-fashioned sinner, wide-eyed and guilty, his head and face looking always on a swivel. She'd tried to explain this once to her husband. A president maybe should have that caution about him, eyes like a deer.

"Deer are rats, and they carry Lyme disease," Marty had said.

Beth sat now with a cup of coffee at the kitchen table and flipped to the back page. Cartoons for today: *Peanuts* and *Lil' Abner*. She'd stopped reading about Charlie Brown years ago. The kid can only fall on his ass so many times before getting the picture and doing something about it, she thought. *Lil' Abner*, though, now this was an important strip, truer to life, the characters and words drawn a little messier, the lines not as sharp. This morning Lil' Abner was messing around on his wife again, with that woman who only hung out with the pigs. But you know what, Beth thought. This was life. He'd go home to Daisy Mae, eat a pot pie or something, and get away with it. Simple. Move on. Be discreet. Daisy Mae loved him regardless, even if she couldn't answer why.

Now, though, it seemed everyone around Beth *needed* to have an answer for everything—the economy, Vietnam, and Jesus, of all things. Well, here was something the news couldn't teach them: the pure courage of ignorance. And ignorant, obviously, is not the opposite of smart.

Marty coughed from the bedroom. There would be a fit for five or so minutes, then a break for about twenty. He would sleep until noon because it was Wednesday, and on Wednesdays Marty was allowed to go in at two. When he woke, he would ask for eggs. If he wanted them over easy, he'd be talkative and excited, point things out to her in the paper, sometimes even make dinner plans. If hardboiled, he'd be quiet and stoic, completely unreadable. But if he asked for scrambled, she'd place them on the table, leave, and sit in the bedroom with the vacuum turned on.

Beth cut open a grapefruit and ate it with her fingers.

She dug her pinky, her thumb, her whole hand into the meat, pulling out strings and membranes. The juices hit her face, and she shoved everything into her mouth until it couldn't contain any more. She swallowed in gulps. With her teeth, she carved away at the inside of the rind. Yes, she thought, yes. It is quite a thing to be messy in private.

Beth cleaned everything by the time Marty came into the kitchen. He wore his robe but hadn't put on his slippers, and he seemed to be breathing through his mouth. He spit into the sink. When asked, he told her he didn't want any eggs at all.

"So what ever did happen to your flan once they gave you the trophy?" Susan said. Just like the discussion of Nixon, the talk of Beth's flan lingered even eight months later. Beth and Susan lay on plastic chairs by the pool. Susan ashed her long cigarettes into empty Coke bottles on the ground between them.

A middle-aged woman brand-new to the trailer park swam fluid, agile laps in the water, barely any splash, back and forth. Susan had her sun reflector propped and held against her chest. Beth wore a large floppy hat to shield her face. "Did they just take it from you? Did they keep it?"

"I guess I was too excited," Beth said. "I never thought to take it home with me."

Susan laughed and kept her eyes on the swimmer. "Well, do you ever worry? Are you scared someone may have stolen it?"

Beth pulled in her legs and sat up for a moment. Why would Susan ask this?

"And what exactly would they do with it if they did?" Beth said. "Analyze it in a lab?"

The woman in the pool stopped against the side edge. She removed her cap and let her hair loose. Completely dry, it fell onto her shoulders, and the woman shook it gracefully off her face. It had bounce. It had a lot of youthful color.

"I don't know what they'd do with it," Susan said. "Eat it, probably."

The woman pulled herself out of the pool, toweled off, and came to introduce herself. Her name was Pat, she said. Her husband drove a truck up and down the East Coast. She had a lot of free time.

Beth pulled the brim of her hat forward so the shade would conceal even more of her face. She didn't say a word, ignored the woman except for a slight hand wave. There used to be a time when she cared about courtesy.

Susan, though, she indulged Pat. It was Susan's nature. She extended her arm and grabbed the woman's wrist tenderly. She explained the dynamics of the park: The owner was very rich but seldom seen. Around the holidays he'd occasionally drive through in his Jaguar and hand out gifts to the kids, always socks and underwear. "It's like he thinks we're all destitute," Susan said. "What a Santa Claus." Susan told Pat about the vandal who'd snuck in on July Fourth. He'd jammed a lit firecracker into the Robertsons' dog, and it blew the thing to shreds. This was Susan's favorite story to tell.

Then, predictably, she described the three major culinary contests: Salad of the Year, Meatloaf of the Year, and Flan of the Year.

While Susan spoke, Beth supposed it could have been possible that someone was studying her flan, picking it apart with gloved fingers, dabbing bits on her tongue.

Susan said goodbye to Pat and told her they'd surely run into each other again soon. The woman walked off without even wrapping herself in a towel.

"If Skipper were still alive, he'd chase her right out of here," Beth said. "He couldn't be fooled. He understood what newness could bring."

"You need to relax and stop being standoffish," Susan said. "Try being nice. Is it something with Marty again?"

Enough. Why did Susan have to pry, constantly pry? Beth could do this too. "How's your grandson?" she said and stood to leave.

The skin on Susan's face looked like it had fallen a little looser. The color had changed.

"His legs don't work, and he still hasn't spoken a word other than 'please,'" Susan said. "That is how he's doing."

Before he'd been deployed, Susan's grandson would visit her every Thursday night. They would eat shepherd's pie. Sometimes, they'd go to the movies.

Well, now they didn't, Beth thought. And that was, frankly, a fact of life.

At home later, Beth had a mop and bucket ready for Marty's discharge. Quite a thing her life was now. When he arrived home, he fell straight onto the couch. He asked for a blanket. Beth wrapped him tightly in a quilt and asked if he felt even a bit better than yesterday.

"The bastard won't ever release the tapes," he said. "You know, the thing about Dick is this." Marty coughed for what must have been two minutes, but nothing came up. Beth visualized his lungs fluttering, black with tar. "The thing with Nixon is this," he said. "The bag of crumbs spends his whole presidency wiretapping himself. He knows he's cornered but won't release the tapes, just to save some face. Well, there's no goddamned face left, Richard. Give up the ghost."

Beth wet her hand in the soapy water of the bucket and placed the back of her palm on Marty's forehead. He wheezed but didn't erupt.

"I'm taking you to the doctor tomorrow, Marty," she said. "Enough really is enough."

"I'll go to the doctor as soon as this rat fink resigns," Marty said. The words and anger were too much for him, and he coughed so intensely he fell off the sofa and lost his breath.

"You're going to die, Marty," Beth said, helping him up. "You're going to die. And I'll have to put a picture of you on the shelf too, right next to Skipper."

"No I won't," he said like someone who didn't even know he was so loved. He had no clue.

◆◆◆

Richard Millhouse Nixon resigned from office at noon. At three, Beth laid out her ingredients for the flan competition on the kitchen counter. By six, she didn't care about either.

She heard two solid thuds from outside the door. When Beth opened it, she found Marty laid out over the trailer steps—his face, the side of his head, his eyes, and his mouth painted with dried blood.

"Beth," he said. "I slipped."

At the hospital, they sat in a fluorescent, sterile room until six o'clock the next morning. The doctor called Beth into an office with a poster of the gastrointestinal tract on the wall. There were newspapers, lots of them, stacked on the corner of the desk—Dick Nixon's face in smudged black ink.

"Keeping them for history," the doctor said.

"What happened to him?" she said. "Marty. And what's going to happen to him?" Beth gripped the right armrest of her chair with both hands.

Next, the doctor spoke in simple words. He spoke truthfully, honestly, tersely. He did not use long-winded sentences or many conjunctions. He paused rhythmically between phrases. He gave her the straight and painful facts, facts that cut and ripped through Beth's heart like a jagged, plastic knife. Marty was now hours from death, and the doctor delivered this news as if he were reading headlines.

Beth did not win this year because she did not enter the flan competition. Instead it went to Pat with the youthful hair. Susan came in second.

Beth ultimately agreed with the decision, but there were certainly faults with Pat's flan. It was a little too soggy at the bottom, and there were bubbles from obviously poor mixing. This would ordinarily be enough for disqualification, but it won on taste. Beth had probably never tried a flan as good, even her own, admittedly. It was quite a thing.

She wanted to think Pat won out of pure honesty, not by hiding a secret, instead letting the ingredients interact properly and naturally. She chose to believe this, to trust in justice, to have faith that pure intentions would always win out eventually.

With Marty's funeral looming, Beth would soon buy a frame to hold their wedding photo, their kiss at the altar. She would place it on the shelf next to Skipper.

But the night after the contest, Beth finally laid her guard down. No suspicions of her were whispered, no fingers pointed. Instead, the three women sat at Susan's dining room table sharing Pat's winning flan with one spoon, toasting to, and yearning for, a better next year and better ones after that. They refilled their glasses, hopeful, until all the wine ran out.

Somewhere Near the Middle of Me

During the date, the third one in a month, the one she said would certainly, definitely be the last, Jena drank too much and again let it slip about her bowel syndrome. Embarrassing. To remedy this, she made up a story. She used to be an apprentice. An apprentice chef for fourteen years in Milan.

The bald man seemed impressed. Oh yes, Jena told him, I can cook. Then—sure—she had to do something so cliché. Of course she had to reach over and rub his thigh. Of course she had to let him take her to a hotel. Of course she pretended to believe he didn't have a pasty wife sitting unaware on the Upper East, maybe waiting for a blackberry pie in the oven, maybe whistling a dumb song about birds.

And he started enthusiastically, like they all did—on top and pressing, squeezing, moving to the next, poking, doing something odd with the tongue. But then he went limp. And this, Jena was used to.

He came to a stop. A bead of sweat dripped from his chest hair and landed directly on her lip. Salty. Gross. Rookie mistake, she thought. Keep your mouth closed, always.

He apologized, the bald man, and said this had absolutely never, ever happened before. She wrapped her arms around him and told him that yes, *sure*, it was okay, and that he could rest his head on her stomach. He did, and the pain in her upper abdomen rode up her side and into her ears.

Jena massaged his scalp with her fingertips. He said he had an older sister who looked too similar, and this made it awkward for him. She got it. After a while, he told her he'd hail a cab.

Jena walked instead, right there, alone, on Fourteenth Street in a drizzle, deliberately splashing through puddles to ruin her damn heels. This is what people did in the city, right, when they needed to think deeply about deep, dark things? No, stop it, she thought. That's movie bunk, you romantic.

On the next one, well, if there would be a next one, maybe she'd say she was an astronaut's daughter. Hey there, blind date, you're only two degrees from outer orbit, she'd say. No, this was ridiculous, too ambitious.

She had a little money because her ex-husband Ron, he put some into her account every week. That's all. Big deal. Who did she think she was?

The day before, Ron had told her to stop calling, texting even. There was no need to bother him anymore, apparently. He'd put the money in. She'd take the money out, use it as she needed or pleased. Ron had been remarried for a long time now. Jena got it. She did, but she still needed him in ways not physical but mental. When her brain was so messed up—too much of this chemical or too little—she stopped caring how many doctors told her how many things, just needed someone to tell her that she still existed tangibly on this planet. Ron did understand, though. She was positive. She'd seen it in movies, in books. You love once, and it never goes away. Everyone knows this.

In her apartment, Jena put some fish sticks in the microwave. She couldn't cook and knew she never would. On her list of things to accomplish before forty-five, this was number four. Well, she thought, too late.

She had to eat the fish sticks now because she had to take the pills before bed (stomach, headache, tremors). They were red, green, gray—all tiny and easy to swallow. One gulp. It was actually comforting because one gulp could make it feel like only one pill.

Tonight she lay in bed without washing off her makeup. She could call Ron again, plead for just a tiny bit of his time. But he lived in Connecticut now, and in Connecticut you sleep at this hour. Your wife's ass is pressed against your side. Your new baby is in its crib with a monitor. And if the wife sees the call, everyone gets so angry. Plus, Jena was too tired and, all right, tipsy.

Instead she sat at the piano. Chords, an endless piece she'd been working on forever. No words, only right-hand melody. This, dedicated to her almost sister. And Jena knew it. Her almost sister sat somewhere inside Jena's stomach now, with sewn-shut eyes, head nodding and hands clasped.

They had shared a womb, Jena and her almost sister. For almost two months. Then a gulp, as her mom had told her—swallowed. Jena absorbed her twin. In utero, the books said. Somewhat common, Jena's therapist said. And this was silly, Jena thought, but they'd have really had a fun time together in *this* world. Shared secrets, shared hobbies. But understandably to Jena, her almost sister now harbored a bit of anger. The burden of carrying the twin caused the stomach pain. Fair enough.

The farther Jena's hand moved up the high keys, the more her almost sister could be heard humming along. She hummed until louder, until shouting.

Ten-year-old Jena stood in the middle of a dry, clay road in front of her childhood house. She stared at the sun for as long as she could, then closed her eyes to see colorful shapes on the inside of the lids, dragons and snakes and such. Once they faded she repeated, over and over, until the sound of a motorcycle could be heard around the road's bend.

This was another deep memory, and Jena was not asleep. Her almost sister made this happen often. Jena was there, through time, in the country again. But she was also here at her piano, in her apartment, in a smothering glass-metal city of sharp edges. She thought of relativity, stuff like time and space. How did she now feel so old and alone, so far away? And why?

She recalled this exact moment. She knew what would happen next.

The growl of the motorcycle grew louder. Jena didn't move from the road. Wow, she was braver then, Jena thought. Naive, sure, but the bravery was commendable, at the very least.

Oh, and here were her older brothers out the screen door, down the porch steps. In this memory, they shared the same face. Jena knew they looked nothing alike, but she couldn't remember how. One had just signed up for Vietnam. Her parents said they'd miss him with the beating of two hearts. How lovely. How terribly, terribly lovely.

And yep, here came the motorcycle. The rider wouldn't see her until the last minute, and she would stand her ground, daring the driver. When he came close, he swerved hard toward the cotton field. The bike turned over, sending the man into the air. He landed face-first and slid for a long time, leaving a trail in the dirt.

Her brother the musician, not the soldier, asked her if she was retarded. Her other brother told him that of course she was, like Uncle Reynold who rubbed his own spit into his eyes.

Jena wanted to enter the past, tell them that, no, she was nothing at all like Uncle Reynold, that she was now paying a Midtown therapist quite a lot of money to assure her she was not like Uncle Reynold, only paranoid. But she was too scared to speak up. Even in her apartment, alone under the covers, terrified.

The rider approached, limping and holding his left arm. He wore a leather jacket, had high cheekbones. His skin was dark. Yes, she remembered, he was attractive. She would have married him if she could. She would have lifted herself onto the back of his motorcycle to ride away until she came of age to marry. They'd live far from here. Far from brothers. In a high apartment building that rose through clouds, where she'd cook for them cordon bleu.

But from the corner of his right eye, blood streamed down his face and dripped off his chin. The left eye stayed shut. He yelled something indecipherable at first and, when he opened his mouth, spat clots of black-yellow.

He cursed. He told Jena to go fuck herself. Hard.

Her brother the musician ran inside to get water. The other tried to lay the man down, but the biker refused. The man looked toward the cotton field for something but shook his head and steadied his bike. He left before the musician came running with a glass.

Her brothers laughed about what the man had told her to do to herself. They said to stay put on the driveway and went into the field. When they came back, they carried a black bag. This is what the biker was looking for.

Her brothers dumped the contents onto the gravel: 8-track tapes. She wanted one but knew the musician would take them all and, out of love, give the soldier whatever he wanted. This time, Jena spoke up and said please. If it was all right, just one.

They laughed again. They were angry that she was so stupid. Maybe if she hadn't almost killed a man, they told her, she'd get to listen. But too late.

Inside the house, she waited for her parents to get home. Her brothers were in their room listening to the music. Jena could barely hear. Finally, they told her to come, and she ran over. The musician said he dug every one except for this piece of shit and threw a tape at her.

He slid the small player across the carpet. She could listen to it but only if she went into the closet.

She took the player and the tape into the small space. Jena clicked the 8-track into place and pressed play. It was a single. *Sugar plum fairy came and hit the streets. . . . Hey, sugar.* . . . No melody. Scary. She hated it then and always would, even now, after thirty-six years and the song coming back into ironic style, wafting like smoke through the speakers of the SoHo clubs.

Her brothers grabbed the player and closed the closet door. They held it shut. Of course they did. They set the player right outside so the sound from the speaker could seep through the space underneath the door. She didn't know which brother kept rewinding the song and starting it over. They probably took turns. And for this reason neither brother mattered again.

A pain like a butcher's knife cut down the left side of her stomach until she screamed. Her almost sister. Her syndrome. She begged them to let her out. Please. She cried, pounded her fists on the wood, then tore down all of the clothes, even the soldier's uniform. Jena had to go to the bathroom. So she did. Right there.

She would never forget this, the trauma of it, the shame in cleaning. She thought of it so often that once Ron had even said to shut the hell up and just get over it already.

And, Jesus Christ, hello, you're still here, she remembered. Jena dropped the cover over the piano keys and ran to the bathroom. She reassured herself none of that was real. Well, okay, it was a real memory. But it wasn't like it was happening again. She stared at the stinging bathroom light bulbs, then shut her eyes tightly.

No dragons. No snakes.

The next week Jena went for tennis in the Hamptons because Ron had changed his phone number, and she needed something new in her life anyway. She knew Ron still loved her, though. She understood why he'd changed the number, what with his wife probably always nagging him, taking up all his time.

And, well, Jena had a membership at the club. Why the hell not get some use out of it for once? Tennis was simple, right? You hit the ball and someone hits it back. You make a friend. Finally, someone as close as a real sister. You have a cocktail, and while sitting with your legs crossed in your white skirt, you laugh with your best friend at just how wonderful it is that you're at a country club and others are not.

But all the women her age already had partners, their trainers or husbands. Instead, Jena got paired up with a girl. And this young, so-obviously-from-the-Cape type girl, with her—let's just say it—arrogant ponytail, simply didn't understand the social aspect of the game. She'd lunge across the court and say there was no way that was out, so don't even think of contesting it. She even suggested, this brat, that Jena consider reinventing her entire approach to backhanding.

After five serves, Jena became too winded. She had to stop. The girl asked if she'd ever even played before and if she'd like some water, lemon or no. Jena dared her to repeat that, to come face to face with a woman twice her age, to look her in the eyes, and to ask such a personal question of her again. The nerve. The disrespect. She asked the girl if she had to be so retarded like Uncle Reynold who rubbed his own spit in his eyes.

To answer, the girl dropped the ball and let it bounce. She pivoted, and when it reached her waist she nailed it. Right toward Jena's almost sister. Right in the gut.

The pain was so intense that Jena vomited. Slowly at first, down her polo. Then a gush of colors sprayed onto her shoes, onto the court. Now, truly, it couldn't get worse. In public, and of all the places.

Jena wasn't asked to leave as much as it was suggested she do so. She had no problem with this. She called a car to pick her up, and when the driver asked what the heck had happened, Jena told him that some adorable little baby had messed on her shirt. It must have been one big baby, he told her.

She changed at home. Online, Jena settled on one man after narrowing it down to three. Not bald. She put on heels, the ones so high they hurt her toenails, and slipped into a red dress. That is short, she said to the mirror. Good. Jena did her makeup like she hadn't done since the eighties. Look at her. Wow. It's like she went through a time warp. She looked just like she used to. Like when she married Ron.

And, oh boy, there it was, her stomach, always her stomach, in the worst moments. She did just get assaulted with a tennis ball, yes? She lifted her dress to her waist to run to the bathroom. Forget the date, she guessed. There was wine here. A new bottle. And really, that always helped the pain.

So she stayed in and drank in her underwear, from the bottle, and it did help. She read a magazine she had subscribed to for many years. But the articles were nihilistic and bleak—politics, the death of the country as we know it, and the birth of hell itself. It tasted so rich, the wine. She opened another bottle, and halfway through, her door buzzed.

She held her breath. I am scared, she thought. I am alone and scared. She didn't know how long people waited after buzzing, but she wasn't going to risk being heard. She quietly pulled a blanket over her face. The world made her feel this way often. Compressed. Choked. Locked inside.

Goddamn it, she thought after a long time, so paranoid. Not even funny anymore. Nobody had buzzed, but now that meant she was hearing things. She should tell the doctor on Wednesday. And she should tell Ron.

At the piano, Jena played the music of her almost sister. Jena closed her eyes and saw the twin, this time unimpressed, angry, growling and smacking her lips. Jena's almost sister clawed at her face, plucked at the stitching that tied her eyelids shut. Jena checked her own hands—right chords, correct placement and key. She stood and walked to the kitchen.

Jena took the pills without eating this time. She counted them out (stomach, headache, tremors) on the kitchen table. She chewed them all without water. There you go, almost sister.

Jena lay on the cold tile and curled herself up at the base of the refrigerator. If she could only close her eyes and imagine being a serpent, she could dance and twirl to the sound of a flute, then surprise—strike and pierce and poison. But now, she couldn't even blink.

Here Jena was, on the rooftop bar of a building downtown. She stood with balled fists, screaming at a man who held his coat up over his head to shield his face from the snow. This was Ron. This was December of '96.

The funny thing about memories, she thought from the tile, is that they aren't really memories of an event per se. Rather, they are memories of the last time you thought of that event. She read this in a magazine.

That was all super interesting, but this was the very first time Jena had recalled this memory, and she didn't want to be here right now, if that was at all possible, almost sister. Please. But the wind pushed the snow against Jena's cheek, and she could actually feel the sting.

The few others on the roof watched as she yelled. She didn't care. She told Ron the only reason she ever married him was that he screwed her better than any of the high school boys. But not true. Why had she said this? Because she didn't like the city. People in the windows, they watched her from every angle, always. He was the one, Ron, who brought her here when they were too young. Now he wanted to leave her. He told her about the new woman. She was an editor. She had a weekly column.

Oh yes, and then what he had to say about the sex. He only slept with Jena—he swore to God—because she was young and naive, and that's what he liked at the time. Girls from her part of the country were so desperate they'd ride anyone to get out, Ron said. He thought she'd be happier here. They could grow and change together. That's why he'd married her in the first place: he felt sorry for hopeless girls. For idiots.

Mostly, now, she thought he had only said this out of anger. But occasionally, she worried it was the truth.

She tried to hit him, but his coat flap was in the way. She slipped on the smallest patch of ice and fell onto her tailbone.

The pain was real, and the cement as cold as the tile she now lay on.

Next: Ron would offer his hand but retract it quickly, seemingly confused about how much care to show a wife one is abandoning. He'd turn and walk through a door that led to the stairs. Jena would cry into the shoulder of a conciliatory woman, accept a cigarette. She'd take a long drink from a flask she kept in her purse, the one no one knew was filled with liquid antacid. She'd lean over the railing and shout to the lighted windows that they all made her stomach hurt, and she didn't care anymore, goddamn it.

Later in the evening, Jena would take the stairs and find Ron waiting for her at the bottom. He had an offer, if she'd please take a cab with him. His eyes showed genuine concern.

From the tile, she knew what he'd say. He would pay for her life—an apartment, food, clothes, clubs, cable television, anything she wanted to feel happy and calm. It was his duty, and he understood that now. But in return, she'd have to see the doctors, the ones whose names had been written on paper and stuck to the freezer door for months. Jena knew that she'd think about it on the ride, that she'd agree to this arrangement, that she'd trap herself in a lifetime of dependency.

"Yes," she said. "Okay."

The sound of her own voice startled her so much it made her spit onto the kitchen floor, her saliva colored from the wine. Red on white.

She should find Ron now. It was an emergency. There was no way, but who else?

And then buzzing at the door. The sound rattled the apartment so much the vibration soothed her stomach, and her almost sister started humming their song. It was Ron. Had to be. He would take her to the clinic. He would get her Valium. He would kiss her and touch her and tell her that she was not, nor would she ever be, like Uncle Reynold.

She unlatched the chain on the door and turned open the bolt. She twisted and pulled the handle inward with an excitement she had never felt in her long, tired life.

Jena stepped out and closed the door behind her. The hallway looked vacant on both sides, and the wall of doors and floral wallpaper stretched into infinity, as if it were a mirror trick.

Ron was not there, and he never would be.

She placed her hand on her upper abdomen, and the twin's music became louder. The melody turned to a monotone and then a ringing in Jena's head until her ears popped. The sound was gone altogether.

Jena's stomach wasn't inflamed or swollen. It didn't hurt. Though the absence of pain did not exactly feel pleasant. It felt better than that. Like nothing at all. For once. It felt like if she chose to, she could walk the endless hallway for the rest of her life without hindrance, into one door and out another over and over again, with whomever she pleased.

Jena closed her eyes and imagined a small girl running from one side of the hallway, laughing and skipping, holding in place a bun done up on top of her head. Jena turned, and from the other end, an old woman limped toward her, those tiny legs determined to carry a body wherever it needed to go, no matter how heavy or burdened.

Would it hurt, Jena laughed, when they'd all three collide?

It doesn't matter, she thought. It's probably about time.

She stepped back into her apartment, locked the door, and walked with an unusual stride past the piano and to the bathroom. She washed her face and brushed her teeth clean of wine. She lay in her bed and adjusted the pillow for comfort.

Jena then fell asleep to the sound of rolling, incoming waves, and in the morning, she awoke gasping, tasting her first breaths of new air.

Debris

I'm speeding south along the East Coast on 95, toward Tampa, Florida. My fiancé, Lea, is in the passenger seat nodding off, and it's making me dazed and overly tired, taillights from one semi blurring into another's, faces forming from smudges on the windshield. Neither of us has slept a full night for almost a week. We're driving to get away from New York and to breathe fresher air, find harbor with my parents.

I veer into the warning strip, the rumble of the pavement enough for me to imagine the smallest earthquake, another tragedy. Lea turns toward the window. I steer the car back into the center of the lane while the country music on the radio drones and keeps droning. I change the station, and a broadcaster attempts to console sullen callers. I shut it off altogether. I'm scared too, really. But for now I'm sick of hearing about shock and awe and retaliation and no-fly zones and a president standing on the rubble with a megaphone. I'm sick of hearing about a city we call home still coated with ash.

I'd chosen the date of the wedding, early fall, September 14, even though Lea wanted spring. That fault's mine. Now the date has passed, the event having cancelled itself, our once eager friends and family terrified, unable to even get near Manhattan. My parents have told us not to worry. Keep the faith. Come to Florida. They've rented a canopy on the beach. Lea's parents have already arrived, ready for our makeshift wedding in the sand.

In the reflection of the window, only one of Lea's eyes is open, so I say her name and tell her I need to talk or I'll pass out too. Her other lid closes, and I worry they will stay shut until we stop for gas. She drops the rosary she prays with every day, for the victims, onto the floor, and I become critical of things I once cherished about her. Her hair is too short. She tugs annoyingly on her ear when she hears a dirty joke. The Saint Christopher medal on her necklace, its optimism, makes me uneasy.

I speak anyway, tell her something in order to hear my voice out loud, a memory, the type that comes back when the mind ventures into the past to avoid the present:

When I was ten, a man called Fuzzy taught me how to sleep a yo-yo. I never knew his real name because, I guess, I never wanted to. He would be a different person to me if his name were Ralph or Bob or Henry or something. In Acorn Ridge, he was Fuzzy—with a gray beard down to his chest, hair that reached his shoulders, and eyebrows so long they curled off the sides of his face.

Fuzzy was a veteran who spent a lot of his time walking the trailer park with a bottle in his hand, looking for change and dollar bills on the ground. For the Christmas parties, my dad would force him to play Santa since he looked close enough. Fuzzy hated it but complied anyway because my dad would take a hundred off his rent for January. So each year he'd put on the dusty suit, spike the cider, flirt with my mom, and tell my dad to go fuck himself.

My family, we lived in a suburb, packaged and arranged for the appearance of prosperity and what comes with this idea. The shiny and waxed SUVs, the homeowners' associations, the side-eyed jealousy of neighbors. All that. And this causes a bit of guilt. Say your family owns a trailer park. The tenants put in extra shifts at the hospital. They work overtime serving tables. They frame the very houses you live in. Meanwhile, you play with the dog in the backyard and get mad when he won't jump into the pool.

Days after one of these Christmas parties, when it was cold, or as cold as Tampa can get, Fuzzy and I stood outside, across the street from the park office. With precision, I looped the string and slid the knot over my middle finger. I dropped the yo-yo and tugged it back into my palm. I could do that well enough.

"Harder, damn it," he said. "Now throw it down harder."

I tried again, wound it, tried again. Fuzzy stood with his arms crossed, a cigarette between his lips, every once in a while saying relax, *relax*, until I threw the yo-yo down and it finally spun in place. It slept.

"Now pull it up," he said. I yanked, and it climbed its string back into my hand.

The old woman from unit 306 passed, wheezing. Her Chihuahua poked its head out from inside her jacket, secretly since there were no dogs allowed. Fuzzy waved.

"Miss Mae," he said, "this son of a bitch just slept a yo-yo for a good ten seconds at least."

"I don't give a damn," she said and flipped us the bird because this is what she did to everyone who tried to talk to her. Except my dad. When late on a payment, she'd call him Sweet Honey.

Fuzzy told Miss Mae that rat and her could both shove it, and he grabbed my shoulder. "I'm proud," he said. "Next, I'll teach you to shoot the moon."

"Can we do it now?" I said.

"No." He lit another menthol. "Go show it off."

I asked who would care, and Fuzzy said definitely not my dad since he was probably too busy sitting in that office looking for ways to screw all the tenants out of money. I said that sometimes, I guessed, my dad could be an all right guy. Maybe. But I wish I'd told Fuzzy then what I'd heard at home. My dad was screwing them out of much more than their money. The Salvation Army had put in an offer to buy my dad out. They'd level the park, destroying what had been family homes for, in some cases, decades.

"Go show your friends the toy," Fuzzy said. "Those creeps will love it."

He meant the kids who hung out in the back, a dirt lot against a fence that separated the property from the nursing home on the other side. I didn't consider them friends, not because I didn't want to but because they looked at me differently. They knew that I didn't live like them, that I had new sneakers every month, that during the school year I had to wear pressed shirts and slacks while they wore basketball shorts. Sometimes I tried to emulate them, but it never worked. No matter how much dirt I rubbed in, everything I wore still looked too clean.

But Fuzzy insisted, and since I *could* now sleep a yo-yo, I headed down the gravel road toward where the kids would be, stopping every couple minutes to make sure I was still able to make it spin.

When I got close enough to see them, this kid I'd never met stood against the swing set, tall and impending, with his arms raised like a preacher, dressed in an oversized suit jacket and yelling. I moved nearer, and the kid paused. I'd intruded.

Melanie from unit 219, the kid who seemed to dislike me the least, pulled me aside and said to check out the new resident, said she would make him her boyfriend and Rico would just have to get over it.

"I can hear you," Rico said, shouting from where they all were gathered.

"Shut up," Melanie said. She cupped her hands around my ear. "Dude says he's a wizard. Like he predicts stuff."

I slipped my yo-yo into my pocket, now hoping no one had seen it.

"What has he predicted?" I said.

She backed away and gestured toward the group.

"Nothing yet," Melanie said. "But if we give him an offering or a present or something, he will tell us how we die."

"We can *all* hear you," Rico said. He pointed a stick in our direction. "Bring Rich Guy here."

Melanie guided me over, and the new kid sat on one of the swings, waiting with his hands folded on his lap, the suit jacket buttoned and pressed. He smelled of my dad's cologne.

"Get this," Rico said. "Meet the owner's son. Makes a million dollars a year."

"My mom told me a billion," Robbie, unit 101, said.

Rico jabbed my shoulder with the stick. "Anyways," he said. "A lot. A ton."

"I don't make any money," I said.

They all laughed except the kid in the suit jacket because, clearly, that wasn't his style. He motioned for me to come closer, asked what I had put into my pocket while talking to Melanie. I said nothing, and he said bullshit, so I said fine and removed my yo-yo.

"See?" Melanie said. "This wizard can make anyone do anything."

"If you give me the yo-yo," he said. "I'll explain your death. The word is reciprocity."

"Whoa," Robbie said. "Rep-ri-top-o-see."

I told the wizard I couldn't give it to him, or I tried to at least. I said that I could make it sleep, that Fuzzy taught me how, and soon I'd be able to shoot the moon. But the wizard demanded. I handed him the yo-yo, and of course, he demonstrated to all how flawlessly *he* could shoot the moon.

Everyone applauded. So I did too.

"You'll die," he told me and rubbed his forehead, "when you are on a battlefield in Virginia."

"This guy?" Rico said.

"You'll have a musket. One of those guns. But you'll take too long to reload. And then pow." I jumped. "Pop," he said. "You will get shot by a Yankee in the back of your head, and your brains will ooze out your ears, and your eyes will be eaten by worms. Also, maggots."

Together, the other kids said hey, okay ew, never mind, no thank you, and they had nothing to give him anyway, what's a musket.

Only a few days later, he walked past me by the park office, following closely behind a woman with the same eyes and nose. He carried a thick paperback, and instead of a suit jacket, he wore a white T-shirt ripped from collar to side, exposing his stomach.

"Rich Guy," he said, and he stayed with me while the woman went inside. He set the book down—*The Flight of Esmerelda*—and pulled from his pocket my yo-yo. "You throw it down. Then you take your left thumb, like this, and move the string to shape it into a triangle. Swing the base through two times, then drop it and lift it back up. That's called Cat's Cradle."

The kid, the supposed wizard, threw the yo-yo to me and watched while I tried clumsily, twisting the string into knots. "Keep working on it," he said. "One day you'll get it."

I would learn it more quickly than he could bet. And I would show him first.

He said, "I'm sorry for picking on you the other day," and stared at his hands as he cracked his fingers. "Melanie wants to know if you'll forgive me."

Just then, the office door swung open, and the woman ran out crying. She fell, cursing in both Spanish and English. My dad followed, saying rent is rent, a deal is a deal, and raised his shoulders like there was nothing he could do about it. My father, not a seer at all, nor a predictor of deaths, but an actual dictator of futures.

The wizard helped the woman, his mother, to her feet and wiped the gravel off the back of her shirt. They walked toward unit 323 to pack their things, and he vanished from my life before I could ever thank him.

Still with a quarter tank left, I'm wiping drool from my chin, so I pull off just north of Richmond to check us into a Motel 6. When I park, Lea's still asleep with her head on the center console. She reaches for me, so I gently grab her hand and tell her, and myself, not to worry. We didn't plan to stop this close to the Mason-Dixon, and we won't stay long. In the backseat are a mix of both essential and useless things we grabbed frantically in the rush: hard drives, unmarked prescription bottles, Lea's box of prayer cards and many pictures of us together and smiling so damn wide, granola bars, a can opener, a set of flares, my wrinkled tux, her plastic-wrapped dress. I lock the car.

The woman at the desk asks if it will be smoking or non, credit or cash. A small television on the wall shows one tower falling, then another. As if time can manipulate itself, the scene resets and the whole thing happens again. I tell the woman that I'll take whatever, anything, just please on the ground floor.

I can't find my toothbrush, so in the room, I use Lea's once she's finished and changed for bed. I lie next to her without removing my shoes in case the fire alarms go off.

"Should we still get married?" I say.

She lays her head on my chest, and it makes me cough.

"That's putting it bluntly," she says. "Yes. We should. And you think so too."

"So have you got in contact with your friends yet?" I say.

"Nope." She blinks for half a second too long. "But I'm praying. And I'm sure they're praying too."

The ceiling moves. It shakes. And Lea tells me to calm down, says my heart is racing. A woman moans. A man grunts. Yes, sex does sound like killing, and coming sounds like death.

"You've got to be joking," I say.

"Ignore it," Lea says. "Let it be. People can still live life for what it is."

"You carry too much faith around with you," I say.

She grabs the remote control from the nightstand, but when the set powers on, it's the same channel as in the lobby. The man upstairs is now quieter, but the woman starts screeching. Shorter bursts, heavier movements.

"Of course I do," Lea says. "Faith is odds-driven. Good things happen more than they don't. Odds are, mostly everyone in the world will be okay after this," she says. "And odds are, together, you and I will be mostly happy."

Lea changes the station and stops on one playing a sitcom, *Cheers*. Ted Danson slides a mug down the bar and gives the camera an all-American smile.

"Do you think Reagan watched this show," I say, "like when it aired?"

We're in a nonsmoking room, but I slide one out from a pack I bought when we first filled up the car, unsure if I'll light it.

"Don't. Of all the times to start," Lea says. "Watch with me. This is the episode where Sam goes on a bender."

"The damn Gipper," I say, "just lying in Lincoln's bed, watching *Cheers*."

The noise from above grows so violent that when mixed with the laugh track, it sounds like the studio audience is involved, encouraging the action, enjoying the show. An entire world gone completely hysterical.

"Put away the cigarette," Lea says.

I crumble the paper and let the tobacco fall through my fingers and onto the floor. I don't remember ever telling Lea I smoked as a kid. So once the frenzied lovers climax and Lea starts to snore, I explain how I picked up the habit in the first place:

The sale of Acorn Ridge hadn't gone through yet, even after three years of give-and-take negotiations. I still kept the secret because I thought if I never told anyone, it might not actually happen.

I spent even more time at the park as I grew up, and Fuzzy and I now sat on the steps of his trailer with sodas, hot as hell from the summer heat and humidity. He pressed the mechanical voice box attached to the hole in his throat and asked me if I'd finally had sex yet. It took a while to get used to Fuzzy's voice, robotic and monotone. But soon, I couldn't even remember how he'd sounded before. My mom, who now managed the park, always made sure the apparatus stayed attached properly, assuring Fuzzy it added character, added charm.

"No," I said, embarrassed. "Don't say that."

"You're fourteen," he said. "You like girls, right?"

"I guess," I said.

Robbie had given me a stack of topless magazines two years earlier. I didn't bring any home—too scared of God and my mother—so I hid them underneath a washing machine in the laundromat. When I couldn't resist the lure of the glossy photos, I'd rip a page out and take it to the bushes.

I smashed my Coke can underfoot, and Miss Mae sauntered by, still always roaming. She no longer carried her Chihuahua. The dog had died, mauled to shreds by two stray Rottweilers.

"Miss Mae," Fuzzy said, then repeated through his machine. "Would you fuck this kid here?"

"Stop it," I said. I became conscious of my skinny arms and growing ears.

"Of course I would, dumbass," she said. "But give it a few years." Miss Mae winked at me and continued on her way, aimlessly it seemed.

"There you go," Fuzzy said. "But only if you get desperate. Trust me."

I curled my toes inside my shoes, shamefully excited, physically, in an unfamiliar and carnal way. Fuzzy asked if I'd do him a favor and unpeeled the wrapper off a soft pack of cigarettes. He handed one to me, nodding as if he expected me to know what he wanted. He pressed the button on his machine.

"Put one in your mouth," he said. "I'll light it. You inhale. Blow the smoke on me. Two times."

It took a while, but finally I could exhale without too much coughing. He closed his eyes and smiled with a look on his face that said thank you for killing me, now I don't have to. The act felt so intimate, I figured I should leave.

I carried the cigarette to the back of a dumpster and sat on the ground, giddy and lightheaded among the loose trash, food wrappers, and a couple dead squirrels. I finished the entire thing, then flicked the butt sideways like I'd seen so many times.

I found my mom in the park office standing, holding the phone with two hands. "And so where is this man?" She pressed the receiver against the wall before hanging up.

"Who are you yelling about?" I said, and she told me it was another one, a prowler, a man who sneaks in to watch the kids play, and I better not ever wander the park again without Fuzzy by my side.

"Yes ma'am," I said and grabbed from her desk my hardback copy of *Esmerelda: Risen* to read at home.

Melanie, somewhat friendlier to me then, had finally passed her driver's test, so late that night, she drove her father's Chevy twenty miles to my neighborhood and tossed an orange against my window. In my book, Esmerelda was balancing on the Bridge of Glass but would now have to wait even longer to cross.

"Get out here, and bring your pellet gun," she said.

I followed her orders and crawled through the frame because I'd do absolutely whatever she told me.

"Rich Kid," she said and led me to the car. "We caught him." I sat on the passenger side, laid the rifle at my feet, and reached for a seat belt that wasn't there.

"Who?" I said.

"You'll see."

Melanie braked, accelerated, fumbled with the stick shift, and we staggered forward.

As we passed tall house after tall house, lawns and fences and rotating sprinkler heads, I felt embarrassed and sank lower into the seat. Here, people owned solid houses, ones built on foundations, the families all perfectly nuclear, or appearing to be, and that was enough. Parents jogged in the mornings. Children rode bicycles only until seven. And every driveway had at least two vehicles, washed and polished, always shining from either streetlights or sunshine.

We took the highway south, and once the palm trees gave way to used car dealerships, then pawn shops and thrift stores, Melanie said my neighborhood looked like goddamned Disney World.

"Have you ever been?" I said.

"No."

"One day I could take you," I said. "If you ever wanted." Ahead, the lights of a motel sign flickered.

"What if I don't need you to take me to Disney World, Rich Kid?" she said. "What if I took *you*?"

I told her that I was sorry, that I didn't mean it that way, Melanie, that she misunderstood, or no, that me, I didn't say it correctly.

She pumped the brakes, scared the hell out of me, and laughed. "Relax," she said. "Stop being so uptight all the time."

"One day, you," I said. "You will take me."

Leaving one hand on the wheel and her eyes on the road, Melanie unzipped my fly. She wrapped her fingers around me. In this suddenness, I forgot how to breathe.

A pickup sped into the left lane and cut us off, and Melanie released to slam her fist onto the horn. She held it until the truck made a left. I exhaled.

"Forget that," she said. "We've got other shit to worry about than your theme parks."

We drove into Acorn Ridge and stopped in the back by the swing set, where a heavy rain had turned a ditch into a stream of water and sewage. The kids stood along this creek, watching something below, each waving wire hangers. Bliss, Rico's six-year-old cousin, sat to the side, her face puffy and wet from tears. I grabbed my pellet gun.

"Here's Rich Guy," Robbie said. "Look at this, Rich Guy."

Melanie and I joined the crowd. A man lay unconscious, his bare feet submerged in the water. A sharp rock the size of a grapefruit rested in the dirt. A businessman maybe, he wore a cream-yellow collared shirt and dress pants—tie, belt, and all. Above the left ear was a deep gash. A large trail of blood slithered down his neck and into the water, where it sank beneath the surface.

"Who is this?" I said.

"Some bastard, touched my cousin," Rico said.

"He didn't touch me," Bliss said and sniveled. "Only as a friend."

"Yeah see," Rico said. "Been trying for a while. We all know it. Finally did."

"So, Rich Guy," Robbie said. "We're gonna mess him up."

Rico's grip tightened on his hanger, bending the wires.

"I guess you want me to help," I said.

"Yeah," Robbie said. "Shoot him in the eye."

The businessman whimpered, and his lips opened like a caught fish.

I knew why they wanted me to do it. They thought it was my fault, my parents' too, for letting the guy prowl around their community. So this was penance, plain and simple.

I lifted the rifle with a shaky grip, and for some reason I thought of the wizard, what he'd said about my death and the muskets, his immense power over us, his returning of my yo-yo and how I genuinely, truly loved him for that. I thought of his compassion toward his mother, his displacement, and his determined faith in the future. His want for forgiveness. Where the hell was he because I needed to show him I could perform Cat's Cradle, and damn it I needed his answer to my question. Would he, right now, here in the muck, shoot this businessman?

"Go now," Robbie said.

"Go now," Rico said.

I aimed and cocked, then turned to Melanie for encouragement, but she now sat with Rico's cousin Bliss against the swing set pole, cradling the sobbing child and kissing her forehead.

"Enough," I heard. The crackle of Fuzzy's robotic voice somehow carried through my mother's open car window. I dropped the rifle, and the kids scattered home except for Melanie, still holding the weeping cousin. Fuzzy opened the passenger door. He strode past me without giving any acknowledgement and pulled the man from the ditch.

"Get in the car," my mom said. "Right now."

My mother drove slowly, didn't say a word. We stopped at a light, and perhaps out of confusion as to how to treat me—a boy, now a little more than that—my mother slapped me across the face. She cried. She apologized, and I said it was fine. I understood.

At home my dad sat at the kitchen table doing something with numbers on a legal pad. He gave me a look from over his reading glasses, cleared his throat, then returned to his work like he didn't give a damn about any one of those kids.

I couldn't sleep. I couldn't read. So I sat on the carpet and arranged my old Army men in tactical position, facing me. I don't know what Fuzzy did to the businessman. Could have killed him, could have saved him. Whatever happened, though, I knew it was just.

The next day at school, between periods, I stole two packs of cigarettes from Mr. Killebrew's desk drawer. With my bedroom window open and the door locked, I smoked one every night until they ran out. I practiced. I watched myself in the mirror and struck poses. One eyebrow up, a sideways glance. Shirt off, maybe jacket on. I mouthed words as if in serious conversation, casual and confident, exhaling through my nose.

That November, my mother would pick the lock and catch me in the act, but she wouldn't care. She found

Fuzzy, she would say, face-down in his kitchen. Dead, almost purple, grip locked on a ceramic dinner plate. Curled up on his back, she would tell me, lay a hungry tabby, purring and clawing into Fuzzy's shirt.

Lea drives through fog so dense I can't see more than a car's length ahead. We've drained the tank twice, and Lea's rosary hangs from the rearview mirror in a constant swing. I fall asleep in Atlanta and wake up across the Florida state line, where the sunlight now catches the windshield and flashes in my eyes. Billboards advertise surfboards, shuttle tours, fighter jet museums.

"Can you get off here so we can cut across?" I say. "I know a way that'll save us an hour, and I'd rather see the swamps than any palm trees right now."

Lea skips a track on the CD player. She asks if I'm sure I don't want to ride the coast.

"More than anything," I say.

She takes the next exit, and we try three gas stations before finding one that's open.

"Four dollars a gallon here," she says. "Price keeps going up."

I enter the store while Lea stretches her back near the pumps, and I only glimpse the headlines on the newspaper rack. Behind the counter, a teenaged girl with a visor and a NASA pin attached to her polo looks at me like I'm about to rob the place, so I walk cautiously through the aisles, grab two bags of chips and a candy bar. I place them down, keeping my hands in plain sight.

The clerk drags the items over the scanner, and I ask for thirty on seven. She types the numbers into the register. To add some lightness, or to remind myself, I tell her I'm getting married.

"Nice," she says and tells me the total.

"I said I'm getting married."

"And I said congratulations." She slides me a brochure for the world's tallest roller-coaster.

"No, you didn't," I say. "You said nice. And nice doesn't mean congratulations."

I catch myself and try to say that I'm sorry, that my mind is twisted by so many things, but she points to my car and covers her mouth in shock. Lea is running to the door. She almost trips when she pushes through.

We watch the guy, bare chested in an oversized suit jacket, tanned to all hell by the sun. He climbs onto the hood of our car and uses the hose to throw gasoline into the air, letting it fall in heavy drops onto his face, his clothing, and everything around. The wizard, it's him, just possibly maybe. He's deciding his *own* worth, his *own* death.

I read his lips. If only for a match, he says. If only for a fucking match.

"Call the police," Lea says.

Instinctively, I reach into my pocket for a yo-yo that isn't there.

Finally, the meter hits thirty dollars, and the stream of gasoline trickles to a stop. The man releases the trigger and throws the nozzle onto the concrete, causing a spark. I wince, but nothing ignites. The wizard lifts his hands in surrender.

After the three of us give testimonies and the man is cuffed, Lea drives up the interstate ramp and says we should block it all out completely, pretend that it never happened, that we didn't almost witness a suicide.

"It wasn't a suicide," I say. "That can't be what he'd choose. He wouldn't."

"What are you talking about?" she says. "That man was clearly harming himself."

A dragonfly explodes against the windshield, and Lea uses the wipers to clear away the guts.

"No," I say. "A faulty pump."

Ahead, a hitchhiker stands with her thumb out, an acoustic guitar hanging off her left shoulder. Lea doesn't say a word about it, probably doesn't even notice the woman. But I pretend we're in the sixties and we *do* stop to take her in. She's headed to the Keys, something about Cuba and the Revolution, but will find another ride after we reach Tampa. She will sit in the back and strum Guthrie songs. Then she, Lea, and I will pull into a rest stop when the sun sets, where we will all make love, kiss each other's stomachs, and with this one act put the country back together. But I was born in '74, too late to know anything about the sixties. This is the bold new century. And the hitchhiker walks in the wrong direction.

"You think that was the wizard, don't you?" Lea says. "The man trying to kill himself."

The speedometer says ninety-three, and the needle is moving up.

"How do you know the wizard?" I say. "You were actually listening to my story?"

"Have you really forgotten how many times you've told me that story?" Lea says. "You are that selfish. You think everything belongs to you. Even the past. That only yours matters. How about this story, *all* our stories—remember when we rented the apartment in Brooklyn, and when the landlord found out we'd lied about being kosher, he tried to hit you with a wooden spoon?"

A bridge raises us over a lake, the water stagnant and spotted with layers of muck. A fish jumps and smacks its side against the surface before slowly sinking back under.

"I do," I say.

"Bullshit. Remember when I landed my first corporate client, when we finally had enough to put down for the brownstone? We tried to celebrate, but you got so drunk on the roof you called me a dyke and said you were moving back to Florida."

"I was worried about the future," I say. "I didn't mean it. Or maybe. I don't know. Permanence, etcetera, etcetera."

"You don't care at all about permanence. You can't make a stand, any sort of decision for fear," she says. "Your past, your past. You're obsessed with your past.

Like you triggered some butterfly effect or something. Like you alone are of so much consequence to the world. Some things are just random, okay? Freak accidents or purely evil acts of violence. They happen. Get over yourself."

In the rearview mirror, I see nothing but empty road, no tourists, no commuters, no evacuees. On the other side of the freeway, there's another advertisement for a roller-coaster, not for the world's tallest but instead the fastest.

"That wasn't your wizard," Lea says. "And even if it was, he was most definitely trying to kill himself. And it didn't have a single thing to do with you."

"A faulty pump," I say. "That's all."

Lea lets up on the gas and speaks for me because she already knows:

You dragged Melanie to the movie theater even though she didn't care about Esmerelda or your fascination with a young princess. Still, she did it for you because she loved you, and she trusted you when she shouldn't have. The Salvation Army had finally bought the property and would soon move every trailer, every home in the park, to a trash heap.

"How long does everyone have to get ready?" you'd asked your dad.

"Once they're notified, two weeks."

If word spread there would be legal trouble. So, even to Melanie, you were too much of a coward to say the truth.

Aside from an elderly couple who must have stumbled into the movie theater by accident, you two were alone in the back. Halfway through the three-hour film, Melanie walked out. You thought she went to use the restroom, but after another thirty minutes you left to find her. The concession worker pointed to the exit.

Melanie sat against the wall smoking underneath a poster for *Beetlejuice*, torn foil and paper from a cigarette pack strewn on the ground. You had asked her to quit, like you finally did after that dream of someone carving a hole into your throat with a butter knife. She never made the effort.

"You want to keep doing these things," she said. "Movies, theme parks, dinners, concerts. But you don't want to talk about college. You're leaving here. You're leaving me."

"That might not be true," you said. And it *wasn't* necessarily true, but you'd been waitlisted at NYU and, if admitted, your parents would foot the bill—tuition, dorm, food, everything. Melanie had a scholarship to Tampa Community. She fucking earned it.

"Just tell me, finally, please, what you're doing in two months," she said. "So I can figure out my own life."

You couldn't tell Melanie because you were as indecisive as you are now, too much of a wimp to make up your own mind and commit to a decision, scared to death of consequences.

The elderly couple hurried past you to the parking lot, and you were angry they left before the movie finished.

"They just don't get it," you said. "The imagery, the world-building, the allegorical nature of the entire thing."

But the truth is, you are oblivious to symbolism. Or you constantly look for it as if the world were drawn up for you by some novelist. As if events were set to be a maze only you alone can navigate.

So you again dodged your responsibility and drove Melanie to Ybor City, where you two would normally gawk at the prostitutes and the megaphone preachers. This time she wouldn't say anything more than *mmhm, mmhm*. You snuck into the bar where they served the underage, but when you handed Melanie a vodka and soda, she boiled over and threw it in your face. Your eyes burned, and a man wearing a fedora, cigar between teeth, said, "Buddy, I know how that goes." Melanie told him to go stick his hand in a blender.

And you were ashamed, scared, that the cigar smoker could be correct, that you would one day be similar, sitting on barstools across America and telling people you felt the same as them. You didn't want to be the same as anyone else. You didn't want your future to be controlled by anyone, even Melanie.

Now, even me, your fiancé.

But you, you got so drunk you stumbled to your car and writhed in the backseat while Melanie drove you home. That's when you told her—once, twice, so many times over—about the sale of the trailer park and how long you'd known. She left you outside your house. You lay at the doorstep. You threw up on the mat.

Melanie didn't answer your calls, your knocks on her door. And when the steel blade of the bulldozer came down on her aluminum home, you almost tried to get in the way, worried that Melanie might still be inside.

Just like that, Acorn Ridge was towed away, piece by piece, shards of scrap metal and glass. Rubble. Dust. Loose chairs, bed frames.

Debris.

You got into school off the waitlist and moved into Goddard Hall on Seventh, the fourth floor overlooking Washington Square, and at the last moment, you switched from French at noon to French at ten. And remember? You almost dropped the class because you took Spanish in high school, and I helped you conjugate *etre*. I couldn't believe you didn't know what it meant.

We sat in the park, to the north of us the Empire State Building, to the south those two Towers so tall their top halves were cloaked by a fleece of clouds.

"*Etre* means to be," I told you. "The simplest thing in the world. Just to be."

And for all intents and purposes, more or less, Lea's telling is accurate.

We're only twenty minutes away. I remove her rosary from the rearview mirror and rub the crucifix between my index finger and thumb. I shut my eyes and examine the carving. Here's a Man outstretched, tortured and desperate. He offers me hope. He suggests I accept it.

My heart expands, glorious, and presses against the inside of my chest. Lea slams the brakes. For only a split second I see the terrified faces of two sandhill cranes, beaks so sharp, unable to lift themselves out of collision with the windshield. I reach and jerk the wheel to the right, and we clip the head of the smaller bird.

There is a thud, and as time slows itself, as we are sent twenty yards off the highway, as the Earth drags us to a stop, I notice how misinterpreted that word is, thud, as it indicates both a sound *and* a tangible feeling. To truly feel a thud, I will tell people later, is to understand you never knew what the word meant at all.

I practically fall out of the passenger side and find one crane lying sideways on the road's shoulder, its legs moving instinctively as if trying to run. There is blood. The beak is missing. I don't know where it is. The bird cries, and while it isn't human, I've heard this awful sound before, somewhere. I grab its wing and slide the poor thing into the tall grass. Its companion circles above.

Lea, stunned, leans against the car. I pull her into my chest, and a long moment passes. She says she is fine, it's just a cut. And it is. Long but shallow along the underside of her ear. To make sure, I ask what my name is, and she says Ronald McDonald. She can joke. She laughs. Holy shit, thank you, I say—maybe aloud, and to God, sure, but also to Lea and to anything else that's ever lived at all.

I don't know why I whisper, but I say, "I did this. I'm so sorry. I chose the route. I turned the wheel."

I hear the flying crane land behind me, and I turn to watch the injured bird stand miraculously. The two stagger behind an oak, and whatever pain and love they share together occurs out of sight.

"Consequences," she says and grabs my forearm. "Listen. We'll be in Tampa before sunset. We'll see family. We might even get married."

She wipes my cheeks, and we kiss for the first time since the buildings fell.

"More likely than not?" I say. "Those are the odds?"

A small group of ants crawls from a hill toward my shoe, and two college kids lean out the window of a sedan to howl at us like wolves.

Tucker and Nancy Are Starting a Rock 'n' Roll Band

After being divorced for ten years with no contact, save for brief moments of passing in the grocery store or the community harvest market, Tucker and Nancy stumble upon each other against the railing of the Carousel Bar at the Hotel Monteleone in New Orleans.

Both residents of Bayrole, Mississippi, they are in town for the World's Fair of 1984—Nancy on assignment from the local paper to photograph the tourists and those who paid the fifteen dollars to ride the river monorail, Tucker for a contemplative weekend alone, which was his wife's suggestion, on the first anniversary of his brother's death. The two collide when Tucker trips over the long derby shoes of a rotund patron and finds himself face-in-Nancy's-bosom. Imagine the surprise.

Nancy can tell from Tucker's complexion that he is embarrassed, scared, and lightheaded from drink. Tucker apologizes and straightens his collar, but a sorry isn't necessary. Nancy is not angry. How could she forget his clumsiness? Tucker orders Nancy a cocktail without asking what she takes because, it seems to Nancy, he remembers many things about her as well.

Tucker suggests a far table positioned next to the stage, on which plays a lazy jazz quartet. A downpour begins, and the room fills beyond its capacity, leaving no escape, so conversation occurs out of sheer compression, then more naturally and with increasing depth. Nancy wears a new summer dress, similar in style to the one Tucker bought her years before, he notes: pastel yellow, a dress he remembers when the nights get too warm for sleeping. Tucker misses Nancy, he does. But he never finds himself pining or longing for anything other than friendship, not for a rekindling, certainly not for romance. His wife and kids are at home in their pajamas at the moment, and they are as precious as anyone's wife and children. In truth, Tucker and Nancy's divorce was without much acrimony or bitterness. We are too young to know what love means and what to supply each other, he had told Nancy on the last night, as they held one another on the bedroom floor. Like dumb woodpeckers, she'd said, banging their dumb heads on wood, trying to find even a little sustenance. They were tired, Tucker and Nancy, of seeking sustenance neither could yet produce. Exhausted from banging their dumb heads.

Nancy softens her posture and offers a cigarette, but Tucker declines. He's quit for his kids, he tells her, and they both grip hard on the stems of their gimlet glasses, simultaneously acknowledging the varied changes that add up slowly over the course of such a separation. Nancy hadn't wanted children, but she didn't know how to tell him then.

She loves Tucker still, sure, but only as one loves kin. Charming, not as funny as he thinks but still funny, quite handsome in most light. Their marriage had started well enough. But they argued over the small things. They each resented the way the other walked, the differing speeds of their strides, the way they used a broom, flossed their teeth. A practice marriage, is what Nancy tells herself. Incompatible but worthwhile for the experience gained.

This meeting, here in New Orleans, is platonic without any question. But if anyone from Bayrole were to know, how the town would talk.

Nancy asks Tucker if he knows she's the town weirdo now, the "one without child," the outcast, the artsy one—she's even heard someone call her an actual witch. Tucker doesn't reply. She's growing tired of the cruel gazes in Bayrole. The gossip. So she has not remarried. So what? No, she does not have children. That's not her desire, and she is now unable, anyway. That is what an illness can do—the surgeries, the radiation treatments. Even still, this does not inflame a *want* for a child; there are days, sure, during long walks, when curiosity pokes her. Gloria, she'd have named her daughter. Or Jeremy, if that need be. But by adolescence the poor things would have fallen down a well because Nancy would have been too interested in other activities than playing caretaker. Nancy pulls a long drag and halfway wishes that, like Tucker, she too would have the willpower to quit for someone: herself.

Tucker and Nancy flinch at every intrusive squawk of a saxophone or clarinet. They've always hated jazz. This music rhymes with you, is what he used to tell her. Too *fancy* for me and *Nancy*. And so, once the rain lightens and they are dewy, Tucker and Nancy skip on a hefty bar tab and find themselves meandering far from the river, toward the deep center of this city, immersed in the evening steam and occasionally grasping at one another's arms for stability over the fragmented edges of the sidewalks.

They reach a warehouse, tall and dented from all sorts of battering, its gate partly open. People, sound, arms tangled and waving. The inner walls are as rusted as they were when Tucker and Nancy last stood here, two years prior to the divorce—that sanguine era—and the music just as loud due to so much reverberation. The drubbing of a kick drum, the relentless velocity and pressure of power chords and distortion. The heat, shared. Their ears burn with spirit.

The band's called Interstellar Glutton, a leather-clad teen yells to them. No cover. The group on stage consists of only two people, a woman on guitar and a young man on a drum kit. The dynamic is rad, Nancy thinks, in a hardcore way. She notices Tucker's own exhilaration in his stiff posture. The band members use separate microphones, and each commands the room with force when one or the other takes the shouting lead.

Tucker and Nancy feel like elder squares, out of place—Tucker with his military cut and Nancy in her wire frames. Even so, they enter the crowd, a viper pit of the sultry local grime, and communicate only through motion and fervor. For hours, with their sweat, out pours their forgiveness, their acceptance, their entire troubled history. The simple idea that many types of love are possible.

"I've got an idea," Tucker says afterward on the banks of the bayou.

"We're not fucking," Nancy says.

"No, of course not that," Tucker says, and they step over a divot in the earth. "Do you still play around with your dad's old guitar?"

Thunder. The night resounds with almighty feedback, the electric buzzing of strings and wires.

"You heard Tucker and Nancy are starting a band?" says Mrs. Lemoine, scissors in hand, to old Mr. Waller seated in the styling chair.

Mr. Waller fidgets, his knees shaking from underneath the tarp. In a little under two hours, the funeral service of his closest friend since childhood will begin, so he raises his left arm to make sure the time on his wristwatch matches that of the clock on the wall. Mrs. Lemoine is the most reliable haircutter in Bayrole, Mississippi, but she isn't the speediest.

"Like a marching band?" he says.

"No, a rock 'n' roll band," Mrs. Lemoine says and snips a quarter inch from above the ear. "A bad divorce, those two, if I remember right."

"I see." Mr. Waller kicks at his gray strands on the floor and thinks of his own daughter, Cheryl, newly wed to an officer of the law. Young enough for marital optimism, he thinks, but not enough of a fledgling to fall for it without caution. "So what does it matter to me?" he says. "I don't care for a woman who is a home-wrecker. I don't care for a man who steps out on his wife."

"You think that's what's happening?" Mrs. Lemoine says. "Look down for me now." She covers the back of Mr. Waller's neck with a steaming towel and presses deeply with her thumbs. She applies the cream, smooths the peaks, the edges. As she does, she cannot help but think of Tucker's hair, always so thick. Yet somehow, his twin brother's had become wispy and fleeting. Being thirteen years older than the boys, she used to babysit them in the diaper days and beyond. Mrs. Lemoine now admits she always preferred Tucker's brother. A troublemaker but a sweetheart. A young, pliable soul. Life is so hilariously brief. A string pulled taut. Why would you want cut it short?

Meanwhile, Mr. Waller combs through the catalogue of his own memories, the reliable ones first. He enjoys the surety of truth, even if traumatizing—the belt whippings he got from his father for cursing, the years of ensuing bed-wetting. The confusing memories are the terrifying ones. Those he can assume are actual but can never know for certain. Did his father really say, "I love you, son," after Mr. Waller, as a child, nabbed that trout?

Then, for a second frightened by a ghost, or just a gust of cold air from the AC, Mr. Waller straightens himself and is nicked by the razor held by the steady hand of Mrs. Lemoine. There is no blood, but both figure there *should* be, so they wait a moment for the oozing. After nothing happens, Mr. Waller says that when there is no harm there is no foul. But before she continues, Mrs. Lemoine wonders how the skin could be so weathered, callused, as if all we humans do is eventually harden.

"You know an old friend owed me a barrel of money before he died," Mr. Waller says. "I won't even tell you."

"That so?" Mrs. Lemoine says. "How much?"

"I said I won't even tell you." Their gazes cross each other briefly in the mirror. "But here's a lesson. Next time you even consider loaning a bastard any money, just don't do it, okay?"

"Okay," says Mrs. Lemoine.

"Here's why," Mr. Waller says. Time clicks closer to the funeral. "Because they'll just go and die on you. They will carry that money with them all the way to the grave. And you know what happens then? You'll never be able to remember them as anything else but an empty space in your goddamned wallet."

Mr. Waller leans backward now while Mrs. Lemoine searches for a more refined razor, and outside a young boy, only ten, walks by the shop window, unwrapping a chocolate candy. He stops when his eye catches the sharp, aged features of Mr. Waller in profile. This head is a planet, and the face suggests a landscape, the boy thinks. Eyes like lakes. Rivers flow within the crevices around the mouth. Eyebrows like a forest, mossy oaks. What lives therein? The chin forms a canyon, and the nose, impending and threatening, purpled from spots of blood, is volcanic. Everyone grows old, the boy realizes, and tonight he will be unable to turn off his bedside lamp, terrified and sleepless from dreams of his own parents' future gravestones and those of all his family and friends.

Mr. Waller pays at the counter. "So a marching band is what you said?"

"No, that's not what I said," Mrs. Lemoine says. "I don't know what type, Mr. Waller, all right?"

"Fine, fine," says Mr. Waller. "Why *did* they ever divorce, Tucker and Nancy?"

"Because, frankly, she's as barren as West Texas." Mrs. Lemoine moves for the broom and tries so hard to recall the last time she's come across Nancy or the last time she's even heard a kind word about her.

"Bless her," Mr. Waller says. "I can't imagine." He leaves. And the bells chime.

Mr. Waller arrives at the funeral barely before the service begins. Inside the casket the lining appears soft. The occupant looks comfortable. After his friend is buried, Mr. Waller pats his face to check for any stubble and then accepts on his cheeks the youthful kisses of so many.

After 8:00 p.m., first there's the heavy Gulf Coast rain, then the pounding fists of hail. Officer Cody Merrit and his long-time partner, Sawyer Dufor, pull off South Main for cover under the awning of a vacant service station, a haven until the storm calms.

Cody brakes too abruptly, and the front wheels churn mud. Recently he's taken to drinking before the night shift, even though everyone knows good and well where that could lead. He's dizzy and feels the turbulence of indiscretion between his ears.

Sawyer, not blind to the situation, hasn't the gall to call out his best friend. They've known each other since kindergarten, kissed the same girls, endured the same hollers of the same field training sergeants. Yet Sawyer has always been intimidated by Cody, by his height, his arm size, his stoicism. The month previous, it took all Sawyer could muster to give it to Cody straight: Sawyer will be up and moving to Phoenix. His wife, Cheryl, is pregnant, and she insists on drier air for a newborn. Good luck and good riddance, was all Cody had said, after all these calendar years. Yes, Sawyer thinks, Cody Merrit's heart is hidden, worn far up his uniform's sleeve.

Cody kills the headlights, and from this vantage the officers can't make out much except for the faint yellow hydrant by the crosswalk ahead. Tonight there's a call out for man dressed like a shadow, seen stalking the alleyways of the moneyed homes here, downtown. Sawyer says it's probably just the Ghost of Christmas

Past and laughs, but Cody doesn't find it funny. It's not even close to Christmas. The officers adjust their seats and lie backward at the exact same angle. The weather won't relent. Tonight, Bayrole is soaking wet.

"So Tucker Mills and Nancy," Sawyer says to his friend, trying again to provoke any sort of reaction at all.

Cody grabs hold of his walkie and turns. "What about Tucker fucking Mills? And him and fucking Nancy?"

Sawyer knew the evoking of Tucker's name would stir the atmosphere. It was Tucker, after all, who'd wooed Nancy away from Cody many years ago.

"Tucker's a college boy. Smug. And always will be," Cody says. "Nancy doesn't want anything to do with me. And now she's a loon and a spinster, and nobody wants anything to do with her either," he continues. "Why are you antagonizing me?" Cody feels within himself the anger that sobers.

"Well they're starting a rock 'n' roll band. Called Shoulderblade or something," Sawyer says. He mimics a guitar, purposely acting a fool. But Sawyer cannot get a rise out of him. "Noise complaint the other night. In the garage behind Nancy's house. They were cutting up with amplifiers and guitars, all that."

Cody takes Sawyer by the shirt, the coffee-stained patch underneath the badge. "That means they're fucking again, dumbass." Cody won't let go, then uses his dominant fist to jab Sawyer on the shoulder with no recoil, hoping to leave a bruise and confident he will.

Just two municipal blocks over and one up, a thin man wearing a sopping balaclava and overcoat endures the wetness, approaches his target location, and hammers in the window of the city judge. He secures his .22 and climbs into the master bedroom. There the judge, a lonely man, plump in his briefs, makes for the door and slips on the hardwood, striking his brow against the frame's molding. *This is too real. This is not a dream*, the intruder thinks. *A mistake. But you can't just walk away and say sorry, never mind, can you?*

He towers over the judge and, as commissioned to do, demands the charges against the mayor be dropped—the misappropriation of funds, the embezzlement, the prostitutes. The judge curls himself like a baby, or a pig, or like a baby pig. He weeps. The intruder fires into the judge's foot, again as instructed, and the judge agrees to the terms. The thin man exits, removes his balaclava for air, and when passing the Catholic church, Our Lady of Continual and Perpetual Sorrows, drenched, makes the sign of the cross. Tomorrow he will be five grand richer, but he fears he will be cursed for the rest of his sinful life. He stops when he spies a police cruiser parked off of Main Street and for a moment considers turning himself in. Then the man in the overcoat pivots to take the long way home.

Hours of silence later, the wind sways the squad car, and Sawyer feels like when he got seasick during his honeymoon cruise with Cheryl. Cody pulls a bologna sandwich out of a paper bag and nibbles long on the corner before swallowing, the way a squirrel would do, the way Sawyer would always josh him for. But now doesn't feel like an appropriate time.

"You can have some if you want," Cody says, and Sawyer accepts the gesture. The bread feels stale in Sawyer's hands, and he can't stand mustard. Still, he chews.

"Why'd you fucking put your mouth where I put my mouth?" Cody says.

"It's a good sandwich," Sawyer says. Already they miss each other. The partners eat in turns, and this is the closest the two friends will ever come to saying *I love you.*

Tucker and Nancy are in a rock 'n' roll band, and now they have the right to say it out loud. Their first stage awaits them on the quad of a state university, east on Interstate 10, in Tallahassee, Florida.

As she accelerates into a different time zone, Nancy commands the wheel and goes over the lyrics in her head. *People, can you hear me? Light your torches, swing your scythes. People, don't leave me be.* Tucker drums his fists and fingers on the dash, and Nancy becomes distracted. Her mind drifts, errant.

She's never been to the Panhandle, she realizes, never been east at all. Always and only the opposing direction, searching, like so many naïve excursionists or prospectors, for something or someone, a lover, or at least a better God than the one she grew up enduring. Three years ago it was a summer in California to put out her feelers. And she had met a few men, a couple women. They were decent enough—tan, oily, porous—but they were hollow on the inside. You could blow through them like you would a whistle. And the place, the state, it smelled of rotten orange peels and copper.

Nancy enters the fast lane to pass a lagging Winnebago.

Tucker reaches into the back to steady his clanging symbols and wonders if Nancy senses his excitement. He tries to emit a little extra energy so to birth a sort of magnetic field and thinks of his family. His son, Tuck Jr. His daughter, Lucy. Fraternal twins. And Rose, his wife—a woman so strong he's terrified to love her as much as he does. They're happy for him, they've made clear, happy for Shoulderblade. They understand catharsis, and they know of his mourning.

A seagull descends and lifts, implying a nearby inlet of Gulf water, and Tucker can't help but notice its resemblance to his old third-grade teacher, Mr. Waller. He laughs aloud from this silliness, and yes, he's been laughing a lot recently. The giddy moments that inflate your lungs. Glee. "If I had to define happiness," his brother once told him, not long before the passing, "it's when you're cackling. When you share a thing with somebody that's so funny your body loses all control, and you can only give in to a great guffaw."

Nancy pokes Tucker's shoulder and breaks the reverie. "What do you think about the rumors?" she says. "Personally, I find them funny."

"That we're remarrying?" Tucker says. "Or that I'm having affair, or whatever they might say next?" When, in bed, he first explained to Rose his and Nancy's plan for the band, she understood with a compact kiss on the neck because of course she would. She is wonderful in the way of nurturing. "Let 'em talk," Tucker says to Nancy. "Each of them will one day have to do something just as strange to make themselves make sense, in their own way."

When they arrive, they find it's a stage in name only. A thin plank of plywood has been laid over the grass for them to arrange their instruments upon. Long extension cords run from the outlets of the distant library. The sun scalds here more than it does in Bayrole, and Tucker notices a thick tributary of sweat forming down his chest and belly. His drum kit won't stay in place due to the warps in the surface underneath. He curses.

A group of three girls approaches, Tucker sees—hair tied and knees showing. A larger collection of boys follows to catch up. Books, bookbags. Tidiness and knowledge. Across the lawn, a football spirals itself in the distance overhead, and all over, there is an aggressive amount of hula hooping.

With three minutes 'til, Nancy awakens her amplifier and tunes her guitar. Her stomach is pitted, filled with unease. She looks to Tucker for reassurance that everything is just as practiced, but he is down to his T-shirt, shaking it open for air. Finally, he readies his sticks for the count and throws her a wink. Nancy announces the name of the band, and Shoulderblade begins well enough, sending the birds fleeing from their trees.

Tucker focuses on the songs and timing, sticking to the rudiments, but can't help assessing the headcount. A crowd of eleven, maybe twelve. They are perplexed, which is at least a better word than bored. Tucker slips into the pocket, finds the grooves in Nancy's riffs. The kids start jamming, feet then legs. Nods and bobs.

Soon, however, Tucker becomes flush. The crowd's youthfulness is disturbed by the approach of an adult man with an eerily familiar gait and stride. This man comes into focus. He stops a few paces behind the gathered students and lifts his leg to pull something off the sole of his shoe. One of his cheekbones sits higher than the other. His arms are thicker than his shins. Bald, you can tell, out of choice. That nose.

Tucker is too spellbound by the doppelganger. The resemblance of this man to Tucker's brother is uncanny, and how could anyone not admit it, or how could they say otherwise, in this moment?

He doesn't remember or hear his own playing until he and Nancy are halfway through their third song. He has fallen out of time, and in his overcorrection, Tucker's right stick catches the rim of the floor tom and snaps in half. The facsimile of his brother, or the imposter even, turns with his briefcase and leaves as he arrived. Tucker cannot describe the pain. He loses his want, then his entire ability, to continue. His joints stiffen, and he stops drumming.

When Nancy turns to see the issue, her mouth scrapes the microphone, and she catches a lip-full of static. The sound from the speakers screams so loud she covers her ears out of instinct, self-protection. The noise won't stop, so she is not surprised at all by the reaction of the student crowd—the hair-pulling, running, and shouting. Just be quiet, she wants to tell them. Why do people yell at loudness? Someone at the library wall flips a breaker switch, and Shoulderblade is shut down. As if they hadn't already thrown in the towel.

Nancy had noticed the man as well, though Tucker is probably unaware, so when she accelerates to join the westbound traffic and the sun falls at last, she says, "Maybe it actually *was* your brother, Tucker. Can you think of it like that? Like maybe he was sent, well, to support you. Give you his love," Nancy says.

Tucker straightens and coughs into his elbow. He welcomes this idea.

"You know what I mean?" Nancy says.

So much optimism, Tucker thinks, is what Nancy has acquired over time. He's glad.

"There will be other shows," she says. "We'll try again."

"We'll try again," Tucker echoes.

After a while, Tucker cranks the window halfway down, and simultaneously, platonically, they feel the seeds of perseverance within themselves take root.

At this same moment, young Father Timms sits next to Tucker's wife, Rose, on a bench in the strobe-lit corner of the Bayrole skating rink—chaperoning the annual youth group lock-in of Our Lady of Continual and Perpetual Sorrows.

Father Timms struggles to keep up with Rose, how quickly she laces her roller skates. The music is Top 40, and it hurts his skull, so he has to shout.

"What's the point of a rock 'n' roll band anyway?" he says. Father Timms knows this is a provocative question. But carpe diem, he sees his chance. How else to initiate conversation with Rose?

Rose points to her ears to say she can't hear.

"Tucker and Nancy," he says. "What do they want with each other? What are they trying to show the world?"

Roses pauses, then pulls her socks high. She's aware of what people surmise.

"Do they love each other? Do they not? If they were to love each other, say, could you and I find ourselves the same way?" Father Timms says. He waits for an answer, then reaches to brush away a fictitious insect from Rose's shoulder.

Rose has felt this adoration, continually, ever since Father Timms transferred to this parish from Boston seven years ago. It's not pathetic, not sweet. Somewhere in the middle, which is to say: boring, tedious.

"You look ridiculous with those wheels on your feet and that white collar," is all she tells Father Timms, and she smiles. Rose stands and pushes herself away.

Dejected, Father Timms sniffs himself, his sleeves. He longs to escape the musky, dank odor of aged chapel pews and confessional stalls. He removes his own skates. Solo and without a hand to hold, he would probably fall anyway.

Even though she and Tucker are happily married, Rose has no need for any man tonight. Tucker is away, and he knows she wishes him well, as odd as his endeavor might be. Her twin kids—nine years old, boy and girl—are in here somewhere safe enough. And so she is free now. This night, for Rose, is about remembrance. Being young. Being alone. Forgetting that the length of a shadow can indicate the unrelenting rotation of time.

Rose glides onto the rink, light as a wasp. She takes long blinks and lets the momentum pull her in whichever direction it might. The music—she doesn't care the style—its melodies enter her veins. Not quite lifeblood but for the moment something almost as essential. Here, her leg rises and bends inward. She dares lift her arms toward the ceiling, and now she's backward, bending around a curve with simplicity. These movements return instinctively, even though this night happens only once a year. But in her mind, she can stretch this night to months, to decades before. Before a husband. Before children. Before joint filing or receipts. Before sex. Sometimes, *most* times, these things are good things. But now Rose billows in the conditioned air, over the waxy floor, and every other stumbling body evades her path. She picks up speed. It's like swimming naked. Or maybe it's like the yearly shedding of an exoskeleton.

To the left of the rink's far railing, next to vending machine, the emergency exit door has been propped open with a pile of gravel stones. The alarm doesn't work, and the three teenagers know this. Down the alleyway and behind the dumpster, they sit cross-legged, smoking cigarettes and drinking liquor stolen from their parents. The two juniors, a cheerleader and quarterback of Bayrole

High, will be engaged to be married in two years' time, they've proclaimed to all who'll listen. Despite their ages, there is no reason not to believe it because in Bayrole marrying young is common, if not expected. The cheerleader kisses the rim of a vodka bottle.

"But we won't end up like this Mr. Tucker and crazy Miss Nancy stuff," she says. "All divorced and turned weird. Stuck here in this one place and acting up with a rock 'n' roll band or whatever. My mom says staying one place your whole life can make you wild like that. That's why she left Jackson so young."

"So we'll end up in Florida," the quarterback says. "Better football. Better real estate potential."

The sophomore, Glen Robichaux, stubs his cigarette and chews on his thumbnail. He doesn't understand what "real estate potential" means, but he trusts it's something about big money. He is angry as to why everyone's so caught up in Mr. T and Miss Nancy's business. He finds himself protective of them, especially Miss Nancy, who, every Wednesday for a year now, has been teaching Glen how to play the guitar for only five dollars a session. It's going slowly, but he's gotten most open chords down, and Miss Nancy's been encouraging him to write his own songs, which, true, has been helping the nightmares and all the clenching thoughts of self-harm. Glen wants to keep this quiet, under wraps, because he doesn't want to be made fun of by his father or his fellow ROTC members, because everyone would think he's in love with a hippie, a spinster. Under Communist influence, his mother would say. But the truth is Glen is just in love with Miss Nancy's hands, the strumming and the picking and how her painted nails so quickly find their correct positions. Her fingers are flexible, and they bend in ways he wishes his could do also. It's a lovely thing, Glen thinks, and so are all the sounds she can make.

A possum leaps off the open ridge of the dumpster and bounds over the laps of the teenagers, causing the quarterback to squeal. The animal was startled by the leering presence of Officer Cody, who now makes himself seen.

The soon-to-be marrieds stay to get their talking-to, but the sophomore takes off, darts fast after slipping slightly on a loose rock. He turns onto Main and only slows once there is no streetlight.

Truth is, it's not like Officer Cody would actually punish anyone. There would be a reprimand but no practical consequence—there might even be some street cred up for grabs. But in fact, the Sophomore, Glen, runs now because he's scared of Officer Cody's sockets and the shiny eyes held within, because he knows by sworn word from his father that these, Officer Cody's, are the eyes that found the lonely body of Mr. Tucker's brother, the reclusive gardener, swollen and tangled in the weeds of the southern lake.

Tucker and Nancy are in a rock 'n' roll band, and come hell or high water, they are determined to keep it alive, their lofty pursuit of self-evident purpose. Their second show is set for today, here in Bayrole, at the Cochon De Lait food festival. They are conveniently slated for 6:00 p.m., just after the sausage-eating contest.

Tucker's wife and kids have been here since the morning to enjoy the day while Shoulderblade stole every possible second they could to rehearse before packing the car. Nancy has never been to this pig-eating festival, not even in her olden days with her earlier version of Tucker. Now, she is willing to embrace the event for the weird and somewhat savage celebration it is. Try it on for size, as they say.

Tucker's wife, Rose, greets them in the dirt lot next to barn in which the dinner hogs have been strung, and Nancy is glad to show off the band's new attire. Tucker's denim jacket has been torn sleeveless, his jeans cut mid-shin. Nancy has gone a simpler way: an oversized t-shirt. But her boots? High. Massive. Rose kisses Tucker on the forehead, then hugs Nancy with both arms. An unusual friendship for Nancy, sure, but they've come to know each other these past couple months, and she'll take a friend where she can get a friend.

Tucker counts a larger crowd than ever at the Cochon De Lait this year. It seems the whole town of Bayrole is present, perhaps out of curiosity. Bayrole's young and old, the butcher of course, the mortician and pediatrician, the high school valedictorian, the dropouts. Tucker surveils the place for his own children. His twins. He spies his son, Tuck Jr., having a catch with the janitor's boy. Tucker's daughter, Lucy, stands not far but alone, staring directly upward and spinning in place as the odd duck she's chosen to be during this funny phase of her life.

Tucker and Nancy haul their equipment across the field, and once they reach the stage, they pause to marvel at the structure. Made of sturdy wood, it sits elevated a few feet from the ground. Four carved columns secure a protective canvas tarp above. Once stood upon, the stage allows a glorious view of the crowd. Nancy lays her guitar case against the PA mixer and turns to Tucker. There's a breeze in the weather, and they feel shaken out of place, jarred loose. Confident. As if from some nook or cranny, they've finally become unstuck.

The bell dings for the sausage participants to start their guzzling, and this causes Tuck Jr. to over-throw the baseball. He and the janitor's kid find it several trees into the woods, where the janitor's kid says to sit because he needs a minute to breathe.

"I saw your dad smooch Miss Nancy," he says, fiddling a twig.

"No you didn't," Tucker's son says.

"Okay fine," the janitor's kid says. "But my dad says they probably did. Smooch."

"Well," Tucker's son says with frankness, "you don't need to be smooching to be friends with somebody."

"I wouldn't mind smooching your sister," the janitor's kid says. He opens his eyes so wide his head almost takes him backward.

Tucker's son stands, says, "Try it. She'll rip all your bones out," and leaves the woods for less shade, more sunlight.

While the sausage champ is coronated by the city judge—a harrowing win for Mr. Waller over the Bayrole Elementary lunch lady—the janitor's kid hides alone under the music stage after prying open an entryway from the back paneling. He's suffocating from romance. He peeks through a crack and locates Tucker's daughter, Lucy, spinning by the roasting pit. He watches until she is called away and out of sight by an adult, or someone older than himself. The janitor's kid pulls from his pocket a box of matches and strikes and blows one after another, reciting the letters that spell out his love's name, L-U-C-Y. As he inhales to extinguish the final match, a surprising, penetrating noise falls upon him. Drums. Guitar. His world becomes an earthquake.

Tucker opens the show with a confident drum fill, and the growl of Nancy's guitar follows. The sounds weave together so well, so loudly, that Father Timms crosses himself with shame after impulsively fiddling with his fingers, tentatively forming devil horns in his Dickies pocket.

Mrs. Lemoine can't understand the lyrics, but the wicked snarl in Nancy's voice awakens a primal instinct in her gut. She locks her knees to create a satisfying tension.

Shoulderblade ends the first song with a crash cymbal and a sustained chord, and in the pause, the quarterback and cheerleader yell for more. Once Tucker clicks Nancy into the next song, the quarterback throws his betrothed on his shoulders, and they wail with the same passion they have for the high school team.

Rose holds her children's heads against both her sides. They nod in tandem and with humming pride. The song is not the best thing she's ever heard, Rose thinks, but look at Tucker go. A husband, a father, and a brother healing.

The Sophomore, Glen Robichaux, who hasn't left his house in days, stands alone by the bed of a pickup. He finally allows himself the release of a pent-up grin. Miss Nancy looks unfettered, her instrument shines red, and she herself glows like a role model should.

Tucker slams the snare. His motions are fluid, and without a doubt, he is loud and in control. His arm hairs stand. His brother's presence. He feels a rush of coolness on the back of his neck, and he doesn't believe in ghosts. But for now, why not?

Nancy submits. To what spirit, she doesn't know. But as her fingers dash madly over the fretboard, she feels the relief of a colossal exhalation. She lets a noise ring out and points to the citizens of Bayrole, and they applaud as if they are welcoming her back into their fold. They are.

The janitor's son, however, is petrified and still. The structure shakes, and the stomping above is like bombs. No matter how much he might enjoy the music, he is losing faith in the integrity of this structure. He musters the effort to move, and his head hits the wood above him. When he frantically crawls through his secret exit, the matchstick falls, its flame catching a tuft of straw grass, and the janitor's son flees and hurls himself straight toward the nearest port-o-let.

Thus, all things considered, Shoulderblade's second performance goes off with only that minor hitch. The fire department doesn't need to be called because the fire department is already present. A quick hose-down, and the flames are extinguished in no time, the casualties being the snare drum and Nancy's guitar cable. Tucker and Nancy have managed to melt the faces of the Cochon De Lait festival-goers with twenty straight minutes of glorious, fuzz-driven rock 'n' roll, and afterward, ex-husband and ex-wife, still intoxicated by the moment, at last hug it out.

Tucker then locates and kisses his wife and kids, big ones, then heads to load the trunk with what's left of his kit. Officer Cody Merrit jogs to follow him.

"Hey, Tucker," Cody says. "The fire looked cool as shit." He twists the toe of his boot. "For what it's worth, just my opinion."

"We didn't intend that, obviously," Tucker says and closes the trunk. "You're not about to cuff me or anything are you?"

"Shut the fuck up," Cody says and holds out a fist for Tucker to bump, and slowly, considering, Tucker obliges.

"You still hit the lanes anymore these days?" Cody says. "Bowling?"

"Haven't in years, actually. Why?"

Cody writes the days and times he's free on a piece of paper, rips it from his pad, and sticks it in the collar of Tucker's jean jacket. "Consider it a summons," Cody says. "In the interest of friendship."

Fifty or so yards away, Nancy is still on cloud nine. She walks the perimeter of the festival to ride the buzz, and after ten minutes she stops at the stroller of a pasty, grinning baby, maybe two years at most. The mother faces the direction of yet another mother, in conversation with probably *another* mother. Nancy asks if, just for second, she could hold the adorable, bubbly child.

Two-year-old Charles has grown used to this by now. Pinch, squeeze, kiss, etcetera. And so here we go again, Nancy with the lifting and bobbing and back-patting. Charles submits, though, for he feels a coziness second only to that distributed by his own momma. Nancy is of the nurturing kind, he can tell—non-voyeuristic, genuine. He hopes this woman might be considered for the position of occasional nanny.

And since Charles is in the recent habit of absorbing information, he takes advantage of Nancy's embrace and views the scene around him from such great height. He takes in the sharp sun, the colors and figures moving in and out of his periphery. Humans of many shapes, mannerisms, and inclinations. The pungent humidity, the claps and whoops and whistles.

So this is what I will inherit, Charles thinks to himself. He spits up a small puddle onto Nancy's shoulder, and she seems amused.

The whole damn performance of the world.

How ridiculously absurd.

Acknowledgments

Eternal thanks to my mother, Angela, for her endless hope and support and kindness and patience, and also to Buddy for the very same.

Writing fiction is a difficult process which always requires the efforts of more than one person. So, I want to thank all who helped give these odd stories life over the last ten years and for the generous editorial assistance offered by the publications in which they appear. I also express my deepest gratitude to Press 53 for choosing this collection to give a home.

I extend that gratitude to the teachers who offered their guidance and saw enough merit in my fiction to put up with my questions, notably Mark Winegardner, who showed me how stories operate (and perhaps more importantly how they don't), and Neal Walsh, who told me to always find the heart and go from there. Thank you, also, Elizabeth Stuckey-French, Rick Barton, Skip Horack, and Joanna Leake. I hope to pass the test.

My endless thanks to all who read early versions of these stories and were willing to share a word or three of invaluable advice, often over a drink, often during the late hours: Drew Jordan, Ferris McDaniel, Jake Reecher, Andrew Siegrist, Adam Karlin, Bryan Washington, Caro Fautsch, Liz Brina, Chris Romaguera, Matt Knutson, Sarah Robinson, Olivia Clare Friedman, Mason Boyles, Tori Bush, and everyone at Yokshop. Truly, your time and thoughtful readings mean everything.

◆◆◆

Thanks also to the following literary magazines that first published these stories, sometimes in slightly different forms:

BOOTH: “Hounds Run”

Carolina Quarterly: “Lucia”

Fugue: “Rag and Bone”

The Georgia Review: “Tucker and Nancy Are Starting a Rock ‘n’ Roll Band”

The Greensboro Review: “Mantis”

Mississippi Review: “Like Always Blooming”

Daniel S.C. Sutter is a 2025-27 Wallace Stegner Fellow at Stanford University. His fiction has appeared in *The Georgia Review*, *The Greensboro Review*, *Mississippi Review*, *The Carolina Quarterly*, *BOOTH*, *Fugue*, and elsewhere. His work has won the Robert Watson Literary Prize for Fiction and the Press 53 Award for Short Fiction. He holds a PhD in Creative Writing from Florida State University and an MFA from the University of New Orleans Creative Writing Workshop. Daniel is from Tampa, Florida.

www.ingramcontent.com/pod-product-compliance
Lightning Source LLC
LaVergne TN
LVHW051002080826
845145LV00009B/2419

* 9 7 8 1 9 6 8 7 8 3 0 4 4 *